IN THE LAND *of* MYTH

ORPHEAN SONNETS

BERNARD KUCKUCK

In the Land of Myth
Copyright © 2021 by Bernard Kuckuck

Tellwell Talent
www.tellwell.ca

ISBN
978-0-2288-4980-3 (Paperback)
978-0-2288-4981-0 (eBook)

TABLE OF CONTENTS

After Damagetus (3rd century B.C.)

by Rainer Maria Rilke

Acknowledgement

I am very grateful for the dedicated assistance offered by my son William who supported me again in all aspects of the preparation and publishing of a collection of my poems.

FOREWORD

Orpheus traverses time and lives in mythical ages, in the twilight of the earliest stirrings of Greek civilization and in wondrous sagas. An enthralling minstrel, he exalts gods and heroes, birds and beasts, flowers and stone, captivating all that he thinks pleasing on Earth and beyond.

In the world of the ancients, poetry possesses a significance it has long lost. Poets are regarded as teachers and holy men, more like shamans than artists in our age. As we attempt to penetrate the night of our cultural forebears in their spiritual abodes, we must consider that devotional status and hierarchy do not always set the tone, that only those seeking, those seeking the highest, soar with ethereal wings.

Orpheus personifies the great dichotomy of light and darkness, being torn between luminous Apollo and esoteric Dionysus, avid to find a divine synthesis which tragically leads to his death. There are certain parallels that hint at the anointed one of biblical prophecy, *Khristos*, no less. A human god walking the Earth and being martyred by those he loves, who miscomprehend his words; a consideration that might have facilitated the Greek's headlong conversion to diverse interpretations of Christianity, one such leading to the seeking of deepest spiritual enlightenment by the Gnostics steeped in numinous thought patterns.

As I arduously tried to penetrate my subconscious to find archetypal illumination in shades of Orphean melancholic stirs, I interchanged the different senses, often letting the visual or fragrant blossom into musical apparitions which play a crucial part in my poetry, where *controlled hallucination* might be seen as *normal* consciousness. Expressed differently, what could be called *a default mode network* makes it possible to focus, a belief in unifying reality – beyond human categories of time, space, and causality, reflecting on the idea that nature exposes only the manifestation of physical existence, not the ἀλήθεια, reality itself, but whose *contours* human thought must, nevertheless, use as essential intimation.

Although I wanted to show in my verses that we humans are universal structures like all matter, as is illustrated by Orpheus singing to nymphs and flowers, birds and stone, that discrete and separate *bodies* are an illusion of our limited sensory perceptions and how these are represented to us by our minds, I cannot always put a Neoplatonic style of ideology into play, since there is an ever-moving meditative penetration of new and enigmatic destinies which is the mark of Orpheus, the epic wanderer who is unable to find repose in any one mystical belief and restlessly tracks along the circuitous pathways of life.

Who apart from Orpheus himself I designated as the purported voice or voices of the sonnet-like forms I chose, which I thought to be potent emotive structures to convey the often hermetical concepts, where soul states matter more than *actual* events, I leave to the imagination of the reader.

Now let us envision a diary-like collection of thoughts and dreams scattered by the breath of Zephyrus and gathered up and read at random, as if the winds of time had stirred again and again in contrasting and transformed ages, for us to relive moments of the enchantment of the golden dawn of a flowering Greece, celebrate the unity of nature and the harmony of the senses, relish the euphoric strains of Orphean hymns, again listen to his enraptured lyre to let our yearnings burn evermore ardently for this blessed land of the past.

Bernie Kuckuck
Longueuil, February 8, 2021

The Tomb of Orpheus

At the fringe of Mount Olympus in a rocky tomb
is where impassioned poetry rested its tone,

the man whose song caused Thracian swordsmen's doom,
made them surrender, who enraptured flowers and stone,

who summoned a herd from the vernal hills,
and forest creatures, flocks of broad-winged birds,

whose lyre according to legend sent forth such thrills,
so deep into the heart of Hades seeped his words,

the dammed fell silent forgetting their pain,
and the Furies could not from weeping refrain.

After Damagetus (3rd century B.C.)
by the author

I

His lyre enchanted field and forest,
gods and mortals, beasts tame and fierce;
birds flying through the vernal skies
were lifted by his melodies.

In quest of bold heroic deeds,
Argonauts driven by his tunes,
at distant Colchis snatched the fleece
from the dragon's monstrous jaws.

Thus from the golden goat was freed,
the ghost of glum and haunted Phrixus,
a triumph beyond the fabulous.

Sailing back to homeland's shore,
Orpheus' mellifluous songs
would the heroes' peace restore.

II

The light I am embracing,
the world of shades I shun;
every day I'm gazing
toward the godly sun.

Up to mountains let me climb,
eye the Aegean from afar
whose waves are in the summertime
twinkling like a dancing star.

In the dim light of the sunset,
hear the siren's alluring song,
the world's vexations to forget,

down to enticing Nereids float,
my euphoria to prolong
or chance on Charon's ferry boat.

III

A gently cushioned golden tone,
a musical magic scarcely grasped,
my lyre's natural resonance
spins out a fervent air.

The Aegean sunrise's glowing spell
a translucent revelation,
the pictorialism of earlier times
unfurling broad horizons.

A sea of deep melancholy
in my autumnal verse
devoted to a godlike man.

Achilles killed – beneath the walls
of fatalistic, splendid Troy –
made me sing a soulful dirge.

IV

The river sings with springtime joy,
marches onward in sprightly waves,
in deep resounding tones,
as a dash of Chronos' time.

Shaded by imposing temples,
I sang deeply from the heart;
a paean of praise to timeless song
proceeded from my lyre's strings.

Where the hilltops said Apollo went,
where ecstatic heights of time
grew out of florid tunes,

I observed the far horizon,
where over the hills of Attica
exalted Aurora rose.

V

I'm dreaming of a spring again
to singing in the treetops listen
and hear the evergreen refrain,
see nature in the sunlight glisten.

A harbinger from Zeus' domain
taught birds and humans how to sing
that virtuosity they might obtain
and exquisite tunes on Earth might ring.

Or is there in us a hidden song,
only awakens when we love,
that springtime passion brings along

hurled by a goddess from above,
to nature's tunes we find the key
when our hearts are vast and free?

VI In the Spirit of Antonio Machado

Sometimes, I feel that love
is pure imagination,
a flaming sunset
of a balmy night in June,

a fleeting hourglass,
a sweet reflection
of your tempting smile
and your sensuous contours,

that it imagines you
and maybe even me,
me who loves!

But could it ever prove
that shadows don't exist
that you, Eurydice, are not real?

VII

Rendez-moi mon Eurydice,
les puissances cruelles de l'abîme.
J'attends ici au précipice,
sans elle meurent aussi mes hymnes.

Mystérieuses ces procédures!
Il n'y pousse aucune fleur.
Enfoncée dans une tombe obscure,
sans espérance je la pleure.

Sur les cordes de mon âme détraquée
des échos tristes résonnent souvent,
les mélodies emporte le vent.

Monde des ténèbres sans pitié,
t'a enlevé mon doux printemps,
pourquoi tant me châtier?

VIII An English Version

How I miss my Eurydice,
powers of the underworld!
Oppressive my imagery
since into Hades she was hurled.

Mystery and darkest gloom
reign in this most hellish place
where never could a flower bloom,
the soul there wanders in a daze!

A distant echo oft resounds
on the strings of memory
that in my heart of her rebounds.

Shadowy world know charity,
hear my song, my lyre's plea,
let me with my dearest flee.

IX My German Version

Komm Eurydike, komme wieder
du aus des Tartarus dunkler Welt!
Höhre wieder meine Lieder
daß dein Antlitz sich erhellt!

Geheimnisvoll und unverständlich
geht umher die große Angst.
Könnt' befreien ich dich endlich
wo du allein im Dunkel bangst!

Auf den Saiten meiner Seele
Liebestöne oft erklingen,
strömen fort aus meiner Kehle.

Von Frühlingsblumen will ich singen,
mit dir durch die Haine fliehen
und immer weiter, weiter ziehen.

X

When in the morning I scan the sky,
I am weary, for I can see
beyond the reddish clouds up high
and wonder what is awaiting me.

Helios' brightness will expose
my body's and my spirit's bareness
that hiding in the shade I choose,
for thorough now is my awareness.

I yearn then for the blissful evening,
harps no longer sound from beyond,
but the stillness is quite pleasing,

and Hera makes my soul respond
to her mist-enveloped cradle song,
for which my dreams forever long.

XI

From the highest tower I watched
the tapestry languishingly woven
over the primeval crossway, spanning
the Enipeus bathed in silvery mist.

Your gleaming, pristine bareness,
virgin of many enticing nights,
more spirited and florid
than Ionia's euphonious wine!

When I saw you plait a necklace
from the sylvan flowers
of Boeotia's mythical fields

in the glowing Aegean sunset,
wave after wave of idolization
stirred in the stream of my veins.

XII

In late summer after the harvest feast,
in the brightest sunshine just past noon,
when Aristaeus from his dream awoke,
the sight of a maiden stopped his breath.

Lightly dressed in a flowery gown
wafting gently in the breeze,
the nymph picked poppies in the field,
immersed in joy and floral bliss.

The satyr whistled, called out her name.
She turned around and, horrified
to be subjected to his force,

she fled in panic, and her feet
trod on a viper in the grass.
The hills sent back her mortal scream.

XIII

The nymph Eurydice, Orpheus' beloved
when pursued by the satyr Aristaeus,
was bitten by Python, the snake of Thanatos,
and dragged to Hypnos' gloomy cave.

The son of Apollo and the Muse Calliope,
steeped in rapt euphonic arts,
strung his lyre and went alone
saying farewell to the rustic scene.

Straight to the inferno the hero drove,
crossing the Styx without delay
to move with his tunes the gods of the deep.

Cerberus with his songs he blinded,
moved Hades with skillful play
and awoke his nymph from eternal sleep.

XIV

A la salida del sol te espero
y hasta que se oscureza el cielo.
Es que, hermosa ninfa, te quiero.
Las olas del mar por ti velo.

Si pudiéramos escapar juntos
a cualquier lugar que fuera
ya te seguiría sin lamentos.
Donde fuéramos ya se vería.

Eres el sol del mediodía,
mi joya, don de la aurora,
hora de la luz, oh cielo, la mía.

La serpenteante via de la vida,
a veces pasa por la mala hora
y deja una grandíssima herida.

XV An English Version

Each day I wait for you at sunrise
and until Zeus conceals the sky.
Since, pretty nymph, I saw your eyes,
with gods and heroes will I vie.

If we could steal away together,
anywhere in Hellas it might be,
I would follow you forever,
down to Hades even would I flee.

You are the midday sun for me,
a gift of Poseidon's joyful waves,
the glory of the Aegean Sea.

The twisting road through obscure caves
will try to cast aside the shades;
the search for sunlight never fades.

XVI

I cannot imagine
where she is hidden;
what Apollo conceives
Hades conceals

in the garden of woe,
where the Lethe rushes
under the pathway
of forgotten beliefs,

where shrieking Furies
frighten blossoming nymphs,
and the dirges of blackbirds

envelop my thoughts
in the shadowy winds
of the unknown.

XVII

Eurydice's beauty the mist-covered world
would not let escape to the light,
Orpheus they sent ahead of the nymph,
never to look at her springy steps.

Thanatos needed Python again
who offered the pair the apple of death.
The lyre crushed on the stony slope,
when in paradise they were to embrace.

The Furies dragged her back into the shade,
her screams echoed in the nightly gloom,
she breathed again the sulphurous air.

No return was possible ever again.
The nymph awaited a cheerless fate,
and Orpheus sang to assuage his grief.

XVIII

The wind is blowing wild and cold
in ragged Thrace where all roads end;
I see the mountain chains enfold
and must to higher grounds ascend.

By the will of the eternal gods,
the deep conjuring of their tunes,
must I triumph over odds
when peril in the ravine looms.

When greyish clouds above are drifting,
my brightest star has disappeared,
the sky's devotion is ever shifting,

it will happen what I feared:
the lonely guest of earthly time
must beyond steep mountains climb.

XIX

The satyrs from the rugged hills
in their euphoria are fettered
by her gleaming nakedness,
by her flowering allure.

They, to whom temptation stirs
at the sight of vernal flair
on the jagged slopes of Thrace,
are easy prey for Eros' darts.

Erratic with reminiscence,
the fierce and unchained river Lethe
sounds a long-forgotten song

when lusty Aristaeus hurries
through the gate of gloomy Orcus,
greeted by abject Cerberus.

XX

Addio le mie care canzoni,
addio il sono della mia lira.
Ad Apollo dico perdoni,
la fantasia me abbandona.

Una volta trovai dei fiori
in un'isola sacra ad Artimidi,
ma quando di nuovo guardai fuori
che il destíno sempre decide vidi.

Però nella mia solitudine,
sento dalle foglie degli alberi
gli uccelli nell'altitudine;

che cantano le mie canzoni d'ieri,
e sento nel fondo del mio cuore
che la magia del cielo mai muore.

XXI An English Version

Farewell, my ardent melodies;
farewell, my lyre's strains;
to Apollo my apologies,
inspiration left my veins.

Once I cherished fragrant flowers
on Artemis' sacred isle;
how I relished blissful hours,
but the fates are volatile!

In my painful solitude
I think of trees in vernal bloom,
of singing in high altitude.

I know my songs again will zoom,
for in the chasm of my heart
blooms the sun-god's sacred art.

XXII

Trees are coming into leaves
in the healing garden.
He rests his lyre in the dim
glimmer of the sinking sun.

The bashful rose hides her allure,
recalling passionate abandon,
her amorous surrender
to midsummer blissful frenzy.

Would that from the shores
of the river Enipeus,
the rushing waves

enrapture the enamoured minstrel
who breathes the scented air of the night
dreaming of his fluvial bride!

XXIII

Lost to the limits of belief,
where in mythical dimensions
fell a fearful deluge of rain,
impacting on the esoteric plan

that a thousand years had woven
across vast spaces of the Earth;
through varying tragic destinies
the world assumed a deadly pose.

The song set out in lengthy trills,
like an arrow flew along the flow
of unchained giant roaring streams

when Phrixus escaped with daring Helle
who rode the unsteady golden ram –
drowned in the flood at Hellespont.

XXIV

Unchained vernal waters
fetter equanimity
in deep resounding tones
with condescending gods,

while tempting river sirens
in the dimming twilight
illuminate their singing
and invent new metaphors,

and the torrential progress
confirms my metaphysics
that all proficiency is will

or Apollonian enlightenment,
the aesthetic, conscious state
of Endymion, or the sunset,

kissed into sleep by the moon!

XXV

I met a stranger on my walk
along the Enipeus' shore;
captivated by his talk
I let my imagination soar.

Countless ideas could we share,
musing over Earth and stars
and how a fire returns to air,
how to stave off earthly scars.

The sun set in the autumn calm,
he left me deep in meditation
with his aura of sacred charm.

Could it be the revelation
that I, the minstrel Orpheus,
had met genial Prometheus?

XXVI

Chantant monte l'alouette
vers le ciel au printemps,
de la lumière en quête.
Mais toujours elle redescend

silencieusement sur la terre,
où elle se repose
de l'hauteur et de l'air
et en moi se métamorphose.

Mais mon vol malheureusement
vira vers l'ombragé Tartare,
où je dois chanter maintenant

que l'Hadès concède mon beau départ
vers la lumière éblouissante
avec ma nymphe transcendante.

XXVII An English Version

Thrilling soars the joyful lark,
ever higher in the spring
in quest of heaven's holy spark,
redescending she will not sing.

When silently she reaches land,
she deserves her short repose.
Whish I could my wings expand,
into a songbird metamorphose.

Unfortunately, I must fly down
to gloomy, heartless Tartarus,
where I shall my singing crown

to move an artless, barbarous
underworld divinity,
to let me with her skywards flee.

XXVIII

Where the sublime heights of time
make the heart feel like an island
in both dark and golden hours,
where the spark of celestial magic

gives zest to springtime germination,
as the cosmos' mind holds sway
over emerald pools and greenary,
moulds a euphoric symphony

where balmy life-enhancing winds
sound with genuine intention,
in sheer Parnassian dimension;

there, the sharing of ripe flower seeds
with deahtless, ethereal divinities
in an aura of eternal bliss,

spins auriols round mortal heads.

XXIX

The evening spreads its shades of gloom,
I'm standing on the hill alone.
Twilight awakes the gods of doom
who want their dusky song intone.

The winds blow ever stronger now;
I hesitate and scan the sky
but must the thunderstorm allow,
its tone will make my sorrow die!

I hear my name up in the air;
the world is drowning in the sea.
What does it matter, Zeus is fair!

The turbulence has taken me
to inner regions yet unknown
where pain and gloom are overthrown.

XXX

Oblivious to the beat of time
under shady linden trees,
by the shore of the Aegean Sea,
where graceful *naïades* danced,

and songbirds covered us with airs
under a splendid summer sky,
like in a wondrous, wistful dream
with marvel and enchantment!

I pulled again my lyre's strings,
drew out a deeply-rooted tone
of hermetic fascination,

drank glowing wine from Aegean isles,
and you, radiant with untamed joy,
sang to praise Dionysus.

XXXI

I have lost all taste for this showy world
and search for a place where to escape.
In order to my life reshape,
let pure elation be unfurled

in a forest by a silvery lake
to hear the songs of dazzling birds
and the soft wind's soothing words.
Would that in Arcadia I could awake

to watch the sunrise every day,
praise Helios, the god of light
and Artemis' earthly paradise,

with naiads dream the time away,
let reveries the sky ignite.
To the gods my songs for sacrifice!

XXXII

Me gustaría una vez más
Tu cabello moreno adornar,
Como en las primaveras atrás
Otra vez ti esperar.

¡Junto al arroyo las saetas del amor!
Que felicidad, que alegría.
Hasta la madrugada … el albor.
Tu eres mi vida, eres la mía.

Pero un día ensombreció el cielo.
Incluso el viento exclamó tu nombre,
Quería morir de desconsuelo.

Mis ojos ahora escudriñan la cumbre.
Ojalá que te manden los vientos
Entre mis brazos por ti abiertos.

XXXIII An English Version

On the path to bliss once more,
your hair with flowers to adorn,
in spring to let my spirits soar,
wait for you to be reborn!

In our world reigned calm and peace;
darts of love spread bliss and joy,
nights spent under discreet trees;
true rapture would the moon deploy.

And then one day the sky turned grey;
I called out your tuneful name,
would to the Sun and Hades pray!

But all my pleas they were in vain.
Wished the wind would blow your charms
again into my waiting arms!

XXXIV

Why do you try to stagger me
with your tempting colours?
Why does the south wind sing to me
engaging subtle drummers?

Why did you awaken my soul?
Alluring springtime damsels
dance in your garden to console,
and your floral dress bedazzles.

Everywhere sprout exaltations,
exotic songbirds hoop above,
in the treetops flourish passions.

The air is filled with vernal love.
I am forever in your thrall –
ever yearning for your call.

XXXV

I recited a *mytoi* by the river Asopur,
appealed to the Muses for inspiration,
to Aeolus to cease the howling winds,
as the siren's song rang from the waves

competing with me, the appointed *aoidos,*
to enrapture the expectant throng,
but rowdy billows drowned my song
and no applause came from the shore.

I put in doubt my earthly reason,
feeling that the wild refrains
had absconded from my inner voice.

The Laistrygonians and the Cyclops
you only meet when hidden deep inside you,
but once I saw Apollo pluck his lyre,

heard the Muses sing on the Helicon.

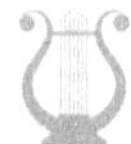

XXXVI

They said a prayer before crossing,
for the coursing stream was holy.
Hear my words, god of these waters,
hear! On my safe return from Argos

I shall offer up a feisty ram, as once
I burnt an ox on your altar,
resplendent Aias, who rules this rushing stream.
Grant your devotee, thus, a fruitful trip!

The bare horizon could now be seen
without an anthropomorphic apparition
like Achelous wrestling with Herakles.

A divine intention lies in the sensation
that greets the flowering in spring,
when nymphs in pristine rivers sing.

XXXVII *The Poet of Hellas*

Only for him murmurs the brook,
the eagle flies to the mountain top;
his marvelling will never stop,
his verses soar from nature's book.

His are the stars in endless space,
Thero's temple in the alder wood.
His holy rhymes are understood
in lands as far as rugged Thrace.

With him the gods of storied Ελλάς
are in steady conversation.
To bestow divine ideas

is his sacred obligation,
but the gods of Hades' gloom
also on his lyre loom.

XXXVIII Im Geiste Hölderlins

Viel bewundert in Hellas' Landen,
die Parzen waren ihm gewogen,
die Götter berauscht von seiner Kunst.
Doch warum erschwerte sich sein Herz?

Am Ufer des wallenden Pontus
besang er die wilde Flut,
und von den stillen Tiefen
sang er.

Er sang wohin das Schicksal ihn führte.
Er sang auf dem Parnass
und im schattigen Tartarus.

Als eine schaurige Woge
den Liebling der Götter erlosch,
hörte man seine Gesänge noch

lange bei Sonnenuntergang.

XXXIX An English Version of
In the Spirit of Hölderlin

All of Hellas treasured him;
the gods were enchanted by his art;
of the Fates' compassion he seemed assured.
What could grieve his joyous heart?

By the shore of the surging Pontus
he hailed the untamed flood,
of its silent depths
he sang.

He sang where destiny would lead him,
he sang on Mount Parnassus
and in shady Tartarus.

When a cataclysmic wave
eclipsed the one beloved by the gods,
his ardent songs

were long heard in the fiery sunset.

XL

Alone I spent a sombre night
in the goddess' forest world,
but deep inside me stirred a light:
a panoramic scene unfurled!

These woods of utter loneliness,
but for the murmurs of the trees,
bestow moments of great happiness,
shun prognostications of Hades,

shun machinations of Thanatos;
unlike Achilles' death at Troy,
my life is dear to Artemis

and shielded by eternal Chronos.
Let Eros' bow procure me joy;
propitious be the ephemeris.

XLI

My endless journeys gave me joy;
like Odysseus I sailed the seas,
travelling home from fated Troy,
steering past the Peloponnese,

lived in the south-wind's melody,
escaped the passions of the goddess Eos,
with final spurts of energy
fled from the Cyclops Polyphemus.

Now let my lyre rule the waves,
my song become a gentle breeze,
that a wistful island craves,

there to sway euphonious trees
and my wrongful death bewail,
with my spirit over vapours sail.

XLII

Now I sit silent and immersed
and watch the crimson sky,
look beyond my love and pain,
look for a soothing phase

while waiting for another spring,
for redolent and tuneful airs,
once more with the Muses sing,
sing in tune with avid sirens.

I have no place to rest my mind,
am hoping for a vernal tone
from Ionia's wistful hills

beyond remote horizons,
to elate my citadel
of utter solitude.

XLIII

Fate suspends
all agonies
by doing battle
with the enemy of truth

blown out of the clouds.
We cannot proceed
with visions of love
like amorous birds

walking the sky
precariously exposed,
unless the gods will meddle,

mediate in birth and death,
in melodramatic schemes
steer us over perilous paths.

XLIV Nello spirito di Anacreonte

Ho viaggiato per le valli di Tessalia;
il mar Egeo ho traversato.
Perfino in Troia ha sonato la mia lira
per incantare i compagni di Achille.

La mia voce lodo Apollo
nel suo templo a Delfia,
e con Dioniso ho celebrato
il vino nobili di Patmos.

Poco tempo rimane qui
per dire addio a Calliope;
il mondo delle ombre aspetta!

Terribili sono le profodità del Tartaro,
e la mia lira non può accompagnarmi;
finché consolare Euridice nelle tenebre.

XLV En el espíritus de Anacreon

Viajaba por los valles de Tessalia,
he cruzado el Mar Egeo,
e incluso en Troya sonaba mi lira
para los compañeros de Aquiles encantar.

Mi voz elogiaba a Apolo
en su templo en Delfos,
y con Dionisos celebraba
el vino noble de Patmos.

Poco tiempo me queda
para despedirme de Calliope,
¡Me espera el Tártaro!

Terribles son sus profundidades,
y mi lira no me acompañará
para el triste lugar animar.

XLVI *In the Spirit of Anacreon*

I travelled through Thessaly's valleys
and crossed the Aegean Sea;
my lyre sounded in distant Troy
Achilles' men to sway.

My song praised Apollo
in his temple at Delphi;
with Dionysus I eulogized
Patmos' spirited wine.

Little time is left to say farewell
to fair Calliope;
the world of shadows calls!

Hideous are the depths of Hades!
If only I could bring my lyre
to animate those cheerless halls.

XLVII

Sleepless night that gods have sent,
silent shade of heaven's peace,
restore to me the stimulant;
let communications never cease.

Send me a token of her thoughts,
for my nymph I stay awake,
I'm praying that a god supports
to let her in my joy partake,

that the stirring heights of time
sweep over the enchanted sea,
that she will always yearn for me,

that her thoughts with rapture rhyme.
Therefore, end my longing night;
let us dissolve in song and light.

XLVIII *The Gods of Hellas*

A part of their splendour remains in all,
in beasts and roses, the inanimate.
In a world so large resounds their call;
their luminosity is the cosmos' fate.

We must not sway away from them;
with increased range is vigour lost
their glitter turning ever dim.
We mortals now pray innermost

that there at last be harmony
between Apollo and Dionysus,
of war and woe the world be free,

the *aletheia* remain their mythos.
To inflame us mortals be their goal;
their spark lies buried in every soul!

XLIX

My ardent songs go fly to her,
heralds of my yearnings be.
Tell her, the most graceful *fleur*,
that her *douceur* bedazzles me.

Loyal lyre, send my love
from my heart a melody.
To watch the waves is not enough;
I want to hold her tenderly.

And let the wind-god blow my airs,
let my singing reach her ears
that she perceives how much I long

to know that she for me still cares,
that she my resolution hears
that all my songs to her belong.

L

The Muses in Pieria graced
his grave with ivy and with roses,
where nightingales the minstrel praised,
and Zeus proposed his apotheosis.

He put his lyre up in the sky;
Lyra adorns the heavenly vault.
Orpheus' fame will never die;
poets will his glow exalt.

His songs are still heard on the river Hebrus,
sung by the loyal nymphs of Thrace,
spreading the minstrel's sublime mythos,

leaving all of nature in a daze.
Tartarus remained a painful dream;
he could nevermore his nymph redeem.

LI

Le son de ma lyre s'affaiblit,
les dieux n'inspirent plus mon jeu;
je me cache de la lumière
dans des cavernes obscures de Thrace.

Pourquoi vous puissants dieux
craignent un chanteur avec sa lyre,
déçu par le destin cruel,
qui se prépare pour le Tartare?

Sur la terre je ne trouve pas de repos,
l'incertitude me suit partout
où les Parques m'emmènent.

Qu'elles me concèdent un été de plus
pour des mélodies sublimes,
pour sonner ma lyre, chanter mes rimes.

LII An English Version

Fading are my lyre's tones;
the gods no longer stir my play.
I'm hiding in a dusky maze
in the opaque caves of Thrace.

Why do you mighty gods up high
fear a minstrel with his lyre,
deceived by cruel destiny,
who longs to enter *Tartarus*?

Nowhere on Earth I find repose;
uncertainty stirs nigh and far,
wherever the Fates are taking me.

Would that they conceded me
one more summer for my song –
to play my lyre fervently.

LIII

I'm looking at the dancing flames
in my cave in Scythia.
I keep thinking of the sandy shores
of an island in the Aegean Sea,

of rustling woods and gentle spring,
sitting on a mossy rock
breathing scented vernal air,
envisioning in a sleepless dream

that you for me would ever care,
that the singing woodlarks soaring,
or the rushing, pristine brook,

that my lyre's longings would,
when springtime magic again returns,
tempt you, nymph, to reappear

in the vanished hills of yesteryear.

LIV

The quiet evenings I spent
in the autumnal twilight,
gentle breezes swaying treetops
by the murmuring brook

that winds through verdant meadows,
listening to old shepherd songs
that blossom in the pastures
of my distant *patria*!

I miss the sweet fragrance
of the golden fields,
my walk through ghostly pines.

The hazy hills of *Thrace*
stir the blood of my heart;
they ever grace my wistful art.

LV

Soaring upwards a thousand miles
as hidden guests of the eternal!
The cosmic mind is holding sway,
sends falcons racing to the sky.

As I pluck my lyre's strings,
the azure confirming expectations
of primordial gifts of light and bliss,
a thousand stars bemuse my eyes.

But Elektra's frenzied dance of death
by the fortress called Cadmeia
earns, me too, the Furies' wrath.

I try to charm them with my lyre,
but Thanatos lights a giant fire;
Chthonian vapers slay my breath.

LVI

Most loved and loyal laurel tree
every year you bloom anew
when your enchanting scent is due,
when the robins sing with glee.

In the garden by the sea
sweet perfumes permeate the air,
but my heart stands still when fair and bare,
a chanting nymph bewitches me.

Her songs spread over highest ground,
in the sky they are adrift,
in ethereal regions to abound

to gods and spirits to uplift.
I pluck my lyre and start to sing;
let me praise this glorious spring.

LVII

Cuando en la noche desvelada
el tiempo al tiempo se suma,
mi alma cansada de la vida,
la felicidad otra vez reclama.

Donde al fondo de la pradera
colina tras colina subir quiero,
hace tiempo, en la primavera,
en la lejana Ionia hallé el sendero.

Como un sueño desvaído,
el mistico aturdimiento
del crepúscolo maravillado.

Volver a Argos yo intento,
por un temporal azotado
solo queda un lamento.

LVIII My English Version

Lying sleepless in the dark of night,
the wheels of time ever adding time,
when my waking turns to plight,
I long to recover the sublime.

Where the meadows culminate
over mountains must I climb,
again to *Traki* peregrinate,
recuperate my lost springtime.

Like a dream in the distance faded,
a mystical bewilderment,
the twilit sky by song invaded!

Return to Xanthi was my intent,
but infernal storms were soon unleashed;
my longed for land I never reached.

LIX

I walk along the road to Thebes
in search of perspicacious Athena,
the magic world of poetry
in clouds that shade the placid moon,

in heaven's golden trappings,
or in a world of silent dusk,
but inside the Earth there burns a fire;
Herakles blocks the gate of hell.

We are fading in a dismal world;
storms are raging in wakeful nights,
all around us shakes and falls,

but the soundwaves of my lyre still,
in mountains and in thunderstorms,
praise bona fide Athena.

LX

I still bear a grudge against Herakles
who slew poor Linus with his lyre
when he taught him how to sing –
impassioned song exalted death.

Bereft of a priori meaning
the world takes on a senseless beat,
darkness embraces Helios' rays,
enslaves the visionary mode.

Approaching storms halt idle chatter,
and whispering in dark ravines,
as time is trembling all around us

and riddles drift toward the shore,
but pathos thought me how to love
Linus' primordial refrains.

LXI

How exquisite was my dream!
I lingered by the Aegean Sea
where pebbles in the sunlight gleam,
where Nereids frolic bare and free.

No gods and heroes on my mind,
the martial splendour of Hellas' tales;
the lighter aerial spirits, undefined,
raised their joyful, carefree sails.

My heart beat an aquatic surge,
when I beheld a mermaid's curves
which would from the waves emerge.

My lyre tuned with playful surfs,
turned songs and verses into charms
holding the sea-nymph in my arms.

LXII

Be aware, Poseidon, weary god;
the sea awaits you eagerly.
Don't let your ever-fading vision
keep you from the frenzied waves.

The land of Argos overflowed.
You empathize with the Nereid's wrath?
Kepheus' wife, Kassiopeia,
cannot match their loveliness!

My prayers will not end, Poseidon;
why not let the Nereids listen
to the playing of my harp?

The sea, the mirror of the world,
with its wild and unchained waves
drowns pretension in conceited dreams.

LXIII

Wie die Geschindigkeit der Töne
Verändert sich so schnell die Welt,
Doch jeder Erfolg der uns erhellt
Verdankt dem Gewesenen das Schöne.

Wir wissen oft nicht wo wir sind,
Gleich wie die Wellen mit dem See
Spielen mit uns Sturm und Wind,
Auch weiß ich nicht wohin ich geh.

Uns zieht das Unbekannte an,
Und in die Lüfte schau'n wir dann,
Doch auch fehlt uns oft der Mut,

Da in uns das Vertraute ruht.
Ich muß herab jetzt in die Tiefen;
Mir ists als ob die Schatten riefen.

LXIV An English Version

Like the velocity of sounds
the speed of change today astounds,
but all success, the most exquisite,
is rooted in the ancient spirit.

The odyssey is predetermined;
like billows on a stormy sea
toys with us the moon and wind,
remaining strong thus is my plea.

We are drawn to the unknown
and often into darkness thrown.
Sometimes we lack audacity

steeped in familiar tonality.
But I must greet the world of shade,
calls from the chasm will not fade.

LXV

Gloomier no night can be;
all my stars have disappeared.
I listen to the Aegean Sea
and wait until the clouds have cleared.

The flowers that at sunrise bloom,
wished they would never fade away,
that my nymph would surface soon
from the billows at the bay.

But maybe I have come too late,
deceived by cruel destiny
stalling her skyward apogee.

Hades might have sealed her fate!
I'm weary of what lies ahead,
that love may be forever dead.

LXVI

To say farewell to Hypata's wall
and welcome field and forest,
silent murmurs tell my soul
in Phrygian lands I must be modest.

To enjoy the flowers of the Earth,
and glancing at life's destiny,
there cannot be a greater worth
than *Poiesis*, godlike creativity.

I'm breathing purest mountain air
where pristine brooklets downwards dart;
nature's charm is everywhere.

But keen desiderata of the heart
draw me to Aegean shores
in quest of fluvial metaphors.

LXVII

Life circulates endlessly
around an unknown fate,
not looking in the eyes
of the weeping sky

but follows the path
of the awakening sun,
scanning its vaulting into
the blood-red sinking,

into the glory of death,
the last lap in the relay
of the eternal cycle,

an exuberant introspective
song of lamentation,
a threnody of divine proportion!

LXVIII

My lifelong search for a connection
(away from inner episodes)
with sky gods circling in the air,
a holy presence envelops me,

best when words are close to silence,
but the Olympians hold their breath
and make me feel endlessly remote
when I'm writing sensuous verse,

although beholding Eos' charms
was even for Zeus a great temptation;
thus, I shall blindly fall and vanish

if I don't transform my song.
I will descend to Hephaistos' forge
to have a potent weapon made.

LXIX

Spesso passo devanti al mare
affinché dirti due parole,
e di nuovo ti abbracciare
la mattina alla levata del sole.

Il mondo mi pare triste ora,
provo troverti ogni giorno.
La sera ti cerco nelle onde encora,
sempre mi desidiero tornò.

Mostra la tua faccia sorridente
ed il tuo corpo quasi divino
nuotando sull'acqua lentamente.

Aspetto un segnale del tuo amore
che finalmente trovi il mio cammino,
e non mi consuma il più gran dolore.

LXX An English Version

I often linger by the shore
to tell you something brief and dear
and hold you in my arms once more;
when will you from the waves appear?

The world seems grey when you're not near;
I try to find you night and day.
Longingly I want to hear
your florid voice. To gods I pray

to see your smiling winsome face,
your enchanting, stellar form
floating on the waves with grace!

Without you, nymph, I seem forlorn,
nor occurs to me a metaphor
to describe my pain, relate my lore.

LXXI

The wars have ceased, the clamour gone,
a world without companions,
solitude, you godless pantheon,
tormenter of my conscience.

But use such words I comprehend;
finally, tell me who you are.
Bygone traumas you like to send
and hide your face; you seem so far.

Let me be without old sorrow;
I'm who I am, I was, and shall be.
Reveal yourself only tomorrow!

What in the waters I can see:
an image of my introspection,
a glimmer of your sad reflection?

LXXII

Free-floating adrenaline,
sudden dramatic gestures,
his fearlessness is genuine,
his chants extol the chasms.

Labyrinthine mountain paths
send his chariot hurtling.
The pathos of freely tempting death
is what we Achaeans call audacious.

With one last paradigm of valour
an epic chanted to the deep
resounding tone of the *kithara;*

the deeply felt *elegeia,*
garland of late summer dreams,
stirs purest intonation.

LXXIII

With the sun's euphoric rising,
my heart in glowing stimulation
plunging into volcanic flames,
audacious Achaean euphony!

But hyperbole of ethnography
in faraway Aeolian lands,
the singing of a tribal song
spreads infernal fumes.

Riding they are three abreast
and cut my lyre's strings;
but fettered in ignominy

their myths and legendary tales,
void of Aegean harmony,
linger in the shade.

LXXIV

The old man stares into the night;
no one wants to hear his words.
Deserted is this holy site
but for a pair of warbling birds.

Ancient columns no longer sing;
silent is Athena's temple.
Argo's eagle has lost a wing;
cast away the transcendental.

Such were the words of Orpheus
whose songs with all of nature rhymed,
but whose death was deemed inglorious

when he a Thracian mountain climbed
and ensnared by zealous Maenads
who tore the genial god to shreds.

LXXV

J'ai envie de chanter
quand le soleil éblouissant
lances ses rayons sur la terre
pour annoncer le midi.

Caché des yeux
est le devin,
et silencieusement approche
le crépuscule du destin.

Quand finalement je te trouve,
beauté céleste,
dans la Mer Égée,

les vagues sonneront ta mélodie,
et les fleurs souriront
dans le ciel du matin.

LXXVI An English Version

I feel like singing
when the dazzling sun
darts midday rays
onto golden fields.

Hidden from sight
is the divine,
and silently approaches
the twilight of fate.

If ever I glimpse you,
sublime transcendence,
over the Aegean Sea,

waves will resonate your airs,
and the exalted sky will bloom
in a golden haze.

LXXVII

A ship laden with expectations,
devoid of ancient tribulations,
gently gliding over the seas,
lets my song live in the breeze.

How pleasing is the glowing sky;
my hope for a golden yield is high.
Melodious wine in my beaker gleams
to celebrate my Achaean dreams

in rustling holy alder woods,
shared with hermetic brotherhoods.
A feeling of primordial joy,

finding the tomb in the ruins of Troy.
The poet's final resting place
leaves me in an enraptured daze.

LXXVIII

The night spreads out
her immemorial gloom,
lingering for eons
in the endless world of shades,

hiding her lugubrious chant
in the bowels of the Earth,
but the twilight awakens
the white and purple morning,

and the Lethe in an ever-deeper depth
with its nebulous conscience,
that the aloof Olympian gods

have forgotten in its infancy,
longs to tumble into the waiting lap
of the primeval Mother Earth.

LXXIX

I'm wandering in greenest woods
where songbirds tweet and flora blooms;
free of the trauma of fateful Thebes,
the sons of Atreus' ancestral home.

The waters of the Areian spring
flow past the citadel Cadmeia;
where Cadmus slew a dragon once,
now nightingales thrill silken tunes.

An aesthetic priest of Dionysus,
I play my harp and love to sing
with Musaeus and Thamyris

in mellifluous, hallowed tone,
in Attica's vernal olive groves,
steeped in the mysteries of Eleusis.

LXXX

The ships regrouped again at Aulis,
but the winds were not to favour them,
due to Agamemnon's kin Atreus who
had not sacrificed the golden lamb to

Artemis who in her anger stalled the fleet.
Omens told them they could not sail
until the king's daughter, Iphigeneia,
were offered to the vengeful diva.

To retaliate for Paris' shame, he
had to transgress and stain his hands,
on the altar spill the virgin's blood.

In the very hour of her espousal,
she fell victim to a vicious rite,
but the fleet could sail and conquer Troy.

LXXXI

Dearest land, beloved Thrace,
far from you I drop a tear
when I dream of your embrace;
magic land, I hold you dear.

How I'm longing for your mountains,
watch falcons to the summit soar
and listen to melodious fountains,
play my harp and sing your lore!

O were I there, beloved land,
in summer when my verses bloom,
the evenings by the sea to spend,

watch nereids from the billows zoom,
walk by the water hand in hand
and surrender to this dreamlike land.

LXXXII

Me asusto cada vez
que pienso en el cielo,
ya que va muriendo
todo a mi alrededor.

Se inquietan mis ojos claros
de que aun en las alturas
extranjero sea
pues en el templo

para elogiar a los dioses
mi voz no he alzado!
Aunque del ruiseñor

el cantar en los bosques aprendía.
Mas una vez, cerca de la cima
me deleitaba el esplendor de Helios.

LXXXIII An English Version

When I look up to the sky,
I feel melancholy
since all of life
vanishes around me.

I'm apprehensive that
even in highest altitudes
I shall remain a stranger
since in consecrated temples

I did not raise my voice
to praise the mighty gods,
although, from the nightingale

in the forest, I learned to sing,
but once I was near the summit
basking in Helios' splendour.

LXXXIV My Italian Version

Mi spavento quando
penso al cielo,
benché tutto se ne va,
tutto muore intorna a me.

Con occhi chiari guardo inquieto,
e mi rendo conto che
anche nell'altura
sia un estraneo.

Non ho lodato i Olimpei potenti
con cantiche riconoscenti,
benché dell'usignolo nella foresta

ho imparato a cantare.
Però una volta, vicina alla cima,
godevo dello splendore di Elio.

LXXXV

Theseus brought power to Athens,
ending the sacrifice
of her children to Minos
and joined the Olympian gods.

At the tomb of Danaos in the valley of Argos
where I rested and tuned my lyre
when I heard that trees and boulders
had followed me to hear me play,

I stood by the hallowed mound
and sang in remembrance of the hero
who gave his name to us, the Danaids.

In the valley, where the river echoes
the sacred songs of Theseus,
my lyre spun melodious wreaths.

LXXXVI

Look into the distance,
Joy seems to have wilted.
Fate's relentless insistence
has frightfully spurted.

Storms sweep through valleys,
all comprehension is torn;
in the flowering heath
a snow-white form!

A silent commotion
pales all that is red
of the sunset's emotion,

Eurydice is dead!
My sorrow surges;
the Muses sing dirges…

LXXXVII

The warring gods and godlike heroes,
the phase of bold inventiveness,
aesthetic, expressive, and phonic appeal,
time has set off as sacred aeon.

But dusky clouds revel on mountains,
love shadows as much as the light of dawn,
and broad-winged birds plunder the sea.
Like the branches of the lofty alder tree

and the wild hyacinth blooming on hills
that resisted the siren's song of glory,
Achilles swore not to fight again

in the quarrels of the house of Atreus,
a passion disastrous and magnificent
that rhapsodized untimely death.

LXXXVIII

Wave after wave his lyre sang,
his passion, flaming into the evening sky,
echoed by mountains and hills;
his odes lauded the life-sending sun.

By the stream in the Aegean twilight,
aroused by the proximity of a sacred force,
the brotherhood of Orphean devotees,
in a gently cushioned golden tone,

emitted a transcendent chant,
a garland of late summer roses
hailing the newly risen star,

arms upraised to the nightly sky
in worship of the godly bard,
that their souls, evermore elated,

join Orpheus on his ethereal cruise.

LXXXIX

Wenn götterhelle Blitze,
by Sonnenaufgang,
auf die Erle einschlagen
und goldene Flammen

im Einklang mit dem erwachenden Tag
in seligem Gesange erschallen
um die göttliche Sonne zu preisen,
lauschen die Verehrer des heiligen Sterns

den Tönen des ewigen Lichts,
denn das aufstrebende Feuer der Liebe
kann nicht vergehen.

Die zeitlose Kraft der Götter
bewegt den endlosen Kreislauf
der heiligen Schönheit.

XC An English Version

When lightning strikes
the divine alder tree
in the morning twilight,
and golden flames

chant in tune
with the awakening day,
in devout praise of the glittering sun,
they listen, the devotees of the godly star,

to the song of the eternal light,
for, the fire of love's passion
cannot be quenched.

The timeless might of the Olympian gods
stirs the endless circling
of sacred splendour.

XCI

I hear the branches call out loud;
the trees are warning me.
It is written in the purple cloud
that from this nymph I have to flee.

When Calypso in her flaming dress
enraptures me with her allure,
I crave an amorous caress,
but cunning snares I must demur.

The stream is flowing calmly by,
the evening ever silent;
flee her temptations I must try.

In the distance gleams an island.
Slowly now the sun descends;
on the starless sky my fate depends.

XCII

Atreus' sons, Agamemnon and Menelaus,
under a warm and pleasing sun,
where rocks lurk under scraggy crusts
of earth in reembracing lands,

recovered from the Trojan siege
and sacrificed to famished gods,
with finest flocks to Artemis
as clouds of smoke obscured the sky.

But the sun went backward on the dial,
revoked the cosmos' axioms;
the orb, great gods, set in the east!

Agamemnon murdered by Clytemestra,
his son, Orestes, slew the queen;
Electra, in ecstatic agitation,

spun into a frenzied dance of death.

XCIII

My cherished lake you look so pale;
why, the plum tree covered you with bloom.
Do you recall last winter's ice,
snowflakes drizzling on your veil?

Or could it be the spectral swan,
with his poignant doleful song
transfiguring your gentle sleep,
when sinking to your gloomy depth?

But the minstrel with his lyre
will wade again on rippling waves,
will forevermore the world inspire

with his rapturous refrain,
his spirit earning fame and bliss
on the timeless billows of his myth.

XCIV

A noble tone flares over mountains;
his lyre dares the starry sky
in beauty and in incantation
guided by an inner sight.

Human triumph over nature
in brightest colours and design,
not lacking grace and fascination
nor ecstatic sparkling light.

Why, even stars are growing pale,
cannot match the constellation
of splendid earthly consecration.

But the cutting sword will deal out fortune
on the altars of covetous gods,
gloat over the *perpetual motion*

of trying to alter the fate of man.

XCV

Mi sento solo quando la fantasia
del cielo fecundo sembra dormire,
tuttavia cerco l'armonia,
della notte eterna voglio uscire!

Ma presto, il entusiasmo ritorna.
Sono come un ucello catturato
chi mai la speranza abandona,
chi alla libertà sempre ha pensato.

Come il fuoco che brilla nell'ochio
dell'eroe quando ha trionfato,
infiammato, un salto fa il cuore mio,

finché come un dio sia esaltato.
di nuovo anch'io canzoni trovi;
per raggiungere il sole voli.

XCVI An English Version

I feel lonely when the imagination
of the gods has gone to sleep,
but soon returns the old pulsation
and new ideas I want to reap.

My soul is like a captured bird
that tries to gain its liberation,
flies ever upwards undeterred
to receive its inspiration.

Like the hero's gleaming eye,
when in triumph he is hailed,
my flaming heart will soar up high

to find the songs that fate has veiled
that in long-gone springtimes lie
and in buoyant mode will magnify.

XCVII

Chronos ruled in early times,
the son of Uranus and Mother Earth
ate his children one by one,
Ogres, Cyclops, and colossal Titans.

But Zeus was saved by loving Rhea
and grew up genial and strong.
He fathered gods and beasts, and Minos,
Rhadamanthis, and Sarapedon.

In the shadowy world below,
Persephone and Hades reigned,
but the *demiurgos* formed

an ideal world from perfect chaos
from the impetuous *Poetic Spirit,*
or from primordial concerns.

XCVIII

Predating the Elysian Fields,
the primeval genius
followed a never-ending
cavernous passage,

imprinting a timeless archetype
in his vaulted grave,
and men, disguised as beasts,
roamed in dusky Scythian woods,

losing their way in labyrinths,
while the scions of Atreus
trekked through arduous terrain,

but the king of Ithaca
tried to find the *aletheia*
in the vast and silent sea.

XCIX

The sky above us moves and breathes
with a race of mighty gods
who form the paramount relation
to the structure of our Hellenic world.

But how can a single *Theos* rule over
an immense and varied universe?
Crossing the rough waters of the Aegean,
from Elaea in Teuthrania, I drifted

ever farther through rugged Phrygian land,
till in the wilderness of distant Media,
I heard a prophet named Zarathustra,

who, draped in a flowering garment,
a *chiton,* spoke with divine intensity
of a unique, gracious god, Ahura Mazda,

who, to make his reign ever more formidable,
was opposed by Ahriman, his eternal foe.

C

A whirlwind agitates the trees.
The brazen stars remove
their inscrutable masks;
the moon flashes its stony heart.

The night is cold;
mist hides the greening valley.
Along the stream
icy flames…

that make the owl
tremble on the olive branch,
and you, nymph of the river Enipeus,

dream – of the rainbow,
of the sunrise,
of spring flowers, of love…

CI

Tu es la fleur la plus splendide
que le printemps peut concevoir,
sans toi la vie parait si languide.
Comme j'ai hâte de te revoir!

Ces jours-ci je me sens si triste,
nulle part puis-je te trouver,
chaque jour je suis une autre piste.
Notre vœu, as-tu l'oublié?

Un jour je passe par la rivière,
le lendemain je monte sur la colline.
Je te cherche, Eurydice, sur toute la terre.

Mais où tu te trouves je le devine.
Tu fleuris dans mon propre cœur,
une rose qui jamais ne se meurt.

CII An English Version

You are for me a splendid flower,
the euphoria of vernal bloom;
I'm looking from the highest tower
to find my *fleur* and end my gloom.

For, now I'm feeling pain and sorrow;
without you, life has lost its thrill.
I'm always yearning for tomorrow;
I will search then on the hill

and check along the rushing river,
will even explore the cryptic clouds.
Our dreams do sometimes differ,

but of my love there are no doubts.
In my heart you bloom forever,
where, Eurydice, you will not wither.

CIII

A spellbound pondering of love
in caves and groves of sacred trees,
in the depths of abstruse seas,
in arcane labyrinths of life.

A fleeting time in Cypris' arms
and Eleusinian mysteries!
Burning passion, sublime dreams
animate in rapt reprise

to celebrate an Aegean spring,
where gods and muses metamorphose
the blooming meadows into song,

there, in ecstatic Aeolian throes,
when holy thunder fills the sky,
to All-Father Zeus we sacrifice!

CIV

A storm now mounts and flags the trees,
and rustling leaves and sparkling waves,
expressions of a willful verve
bring an end to the harvest feast,

a somewhat euphemistic genus
and a hypostasis of previous worlds,
a joy too bright and ravishing
for his sober Achaean kin.

Pillars of cedar, laurels, and valour
pressing forward toward grace,
from the shadows bearing torches

but remain in the chrysalis stage.
Orpheus hails the rainbow
and the dancing flame,

in tempests and the trembling Earth
envisions a transcendent plan.

CV

On the toilsome road to Lydia
by the Pactolus River's shore
and motioned by the twilight's musings,
I heard the wistful sirens sing

my song of earthly destiny,
assume an ever-downward course,
like the pristine waters of a source,
dropping down from cliff to cliff

onto tearful sylvan bloom,
weeping out of vernal joy
or of looming autumnal woe,

weep for the days of bygone wonder,
weep of rapture or despair,
of uncertainty that I must bear.

CVI

I like to sail to distant lands,
but it's late to trail Odysseus,
find the path where sorrow ends,
attain the most vainglorious.

I'm searching for a world profound
where they grasp veracious art.
The road might not be always kind
but must not circumvent my heart.

I am soaring now above the stars,
my eyes beholding from up high
me, Orpheus, with all my scars,

breathing songs to the mighty sky,
in a night so true and clear –
still far from my envisioned sphere!

CVII

Cielo estrellado extraño,
donde las sombras de nuestros héroes
vagan para descubrir cuentas oscuras
y mitos y leyendas,

y melodías sin rayos del sol,
que ni siquiera el sombrío Hades,
en su edad primigenia,
hubiera podido imaginar,

enigmas oscuros inconcebibles
que se expanden sin fin,
visto por el ojo ciego

del buscador de la *aletheia*
que atraviesa el muro inpenetrable,
el único camino hacia el *absoluto*.

CVIII An English Version

Strange star-studded space
where the heroes' restless spirits
make their shadows roam
to appear in gloomy legends

and myths without a melody
that not even cheerless Hades,
in his earlier cycles,
could have conceived,

dark incommunicable enigmas,
ever expanding, seen with the blind eye
of the seeker of the *aletheia,*

who smashes the gate
of the impenetrable wall,
the only roadway to the gods.

CIX

It has no beginning, will endlessly flame,
the light that forever seeks the shade,
pursues the unfolding of Orphic rites
extolling the mystery of Dionysus,

the suffering god, whose paling image
submerged without the sounding
of an elegy by the howling storms,
the Neptunian trumpets that continue

to reign over the darkly roaring sea
beyond the vast extent of silence,
beyond the oracle of Delos,

but the mysteries of life and death
that shine between the rocking waves
wade toward a hallowed shore,

toward a solemn interlude.

CX

Songs of my feelings and reflections,
thrilling devotees with the sound
of burning passion that enflames the mind,
are conceived to stir the imagination

of man for a mystery to be resolved.
The atoms of arithmetic, prime numbers,
the building blocks of all that *counts,*
take us on a stunning journey

into the arcane world of sounds
to solve the greatest enigma,
the very life beyond the grave.

These vexing numbers rhyme with chaos,
the purest of poetic forms
circling in the hearts of dreamers,

looking for mysterious norms.

CXI *The Aletheia*

Where shadows drift over Aegean strands
and through the stillness sings the sea,
veiled in timeless garb you wander
in Helios' light with certain steps.

The *sophists* of the *Peloponnesus*
felt the lustre of your spark;
the ancients called you *αληθεια*,
your friendship was their noblest quest.

But you go about in silence,
unrecognized by mortal man;
just a few will grasp your science,

relishing your arcane glow,
endure the chilly winds that blow
against your magic from the void.

CXII

I wandered by the vernal shore
of the river Eridanus
waiting for a magic wave
to divulge a naiad

with flowering Achaean hair.
Euphoric springtime longing
heard her alluring chant
when the willow branches stirred,

and the ghostly shades conferred
the awaited nymph-like form
in the pristine stream.

The animated windswept waves
echoed the arboreal song
of the trembling spectral willows.

CXIII

Müde von meinen langen Reisen,
fand ich Ruhe unter einem schattigen Baum.
Die alten Schäfer sangen noch die Weisen
von der Bergnymphe im Sonnentraum,

die durch Apollo in Lorbeer verbannte.
Die züchtige Priesterin der Göttin Erde,
die nur die Liebe für die Blumen kannte,
achtete nicht des Gottes glühender Gebärde.

Beim Rebenfest des Dionysus
gewann ich den Lorbeer mit der Leier
und von der Nymphe einen zarten Kuß.

Daphne liebt das Licht und nicht das Feuer.
Im Traum hörte ich noch Saitenklang
und der Baum ein süßes Lied mir sang.

CXIV An English Version

Exhausted from my endless travels,
I rested under a shady laurel.
The old shepherds by the river Tempe
sang songs about a mountain nymph.

Pursued by the god Apollo,
made her morph into a tree.
The priestess of the goddess Earth
felt love for trees and flowers

but no passion for the flaming sun.
Daphne loves the light but not the fire!
At Dionysus' summer celebration,

I won the laurels with my lyre!
I still dream about this magic day,
whistling her tune I go my way.

CXV

Nothing can worsen the image unseen
arising beyond the Ionian Sea
that is carried by innocent clouds,
driven by enigmatic whirlwinds of fate.

A silent death spreads from Miletus,
changes direction out of sheer will.
The bewildered waves gather again:
the wrath of destiny's cruel act.

Thousands of fighters cannot control
the anger of the chthonian gods.
The *phrostries* of Megara on the Isthmus

lift their swords in daring dismay,
ready to slash the shadows of hell
their Dorian valour cannot delay.

CXVI

…pero vientos calurosos pasan
encima del Mar Ageo –
Ninfas de las aguas profundas
atraviesan escombros de carruajes

planeadores de *Neofaetones*
cayendo en cuanto asaltan el cielo.
Luminarias, cada vez menos intensas
elogian sus alas de águila imaginaria,

y vapores de la mañana se extienden
más allá de revelaciones antiguas,
penetran en los cráneos serenos

de épocas atrevidas
en sus odiseas
hacia la fuente del tiempo.

CXVII An English Version

… but heated winds sweep
over the Aegean Sea –
Deep-water nymphs wade
through the falling debris

of the soaring carriages
of sky storming *Neo-Phaetons.*
Dwindling luminaries
still shower praise

on their imagined eagle wings,
and morning vapours spread
over ancient revelations,

penetrating the skulls
of venturesome ages
on their restive journeys

toward the beginning of time.

CXVIII

Come i fiori delle nubi argentati,
il canto alletante delle sirene
passa sopra il Mar Ionio,
una brezza leggere e meravigliosa

procede dell' isola favalosa.
La rosa crece selvaticamente qui,
dove i poeti sono semidei,
le muse cantano canti incantevoli,

dove le rocce sovastrano il mare,
le ninfe vogliono con le onde ballare.
Le colline d'Itaca in fiore,

desseminano dei lillà sopra il Styx
che tutti i mortali attraversano,
ma del traghettatore Caronte si fidano.

CXIX An English Version

Like the blossoming motley clouds
glistening over the Ionian Sea,
gently drifts the sirens' song,
a mellow breeze from storied Greece,

land of gods and the golden fleece.
The rose grows wild on fabled isles
where poets thrive and Muses sing,
and bees hum in the summer glow,

where mountains overhang the sea,
enchanting nymphs romp bare and free.
The mythic land in purple bloom

strews lilacs on the river Styx,
across which all we mortals course
but trust in Charon's *tour de force.*

CXX

Don't think that my songs
always rhyme with tales
extolling heroic deeds
brought back from distant shores.

The distance between my verses
and the reality of my ventures
has become vague.
I sing them the way I remember.

But you can be certain that I saw
the gods of darkness weep
when Orpheus played his lyre

in the ghostly halls of Hades –
or in the very atom's heart – where
I used to linger in primordial times.

CXXI

Providing protection from war, sieges, and wrath,
strong walls shielded the keeps of kings,
adorned with hallow symbols
of the ever-rising and unconquered sun.

The *potamoi,* gods of rivers and streams,
demanded sacrifice from the *strategos*
and his army of vainglorious *hoplites,*
as they tried to cross over the Hebrus.

They offered the corpses of fierce enemies,
when they heard the sirens' ballads of war,
but drowned in the river's untamed waves.

He was grateful, the king of Thrace
whose men burnt the hides of a hundred steers,
thanking Alpheiros for sinking his foes.

CXXII

By the rock fortress of Paeonia
to celebrate the vernal equinox,
the rapt ancient revelries,
evocative flares of primordial lore,

enhanced by animated dreams
at the point of deepest transport,
neither sun, nor moon, nor the
enlightened stars, not even the rising

flames of my reawakened joy
could match the enchantment
extended by the phenomenon

of the heralding golden falcon
soaring up to lofty heights,
auguring a plethora of bliss.

CXXIII

Tomo el camino de los sueños,
por los cipreses blancos
donde vive mi pasión
en las noches de llena luna.

En la penumbra del amanecer
se pone a cantar el viento;
por el aire de la mañana
el dulce silbido de flautas,

y de la sombra ha surgido
el marchito palacio de piedra
donde los rosales propagan aún

sus aromas de tiempos remotos,
donde una princesa en su sueño profundo
me espera para réanimar su aliento.

CXXIV An English Version

I follow the road of my dreams,
shaded by white cypresses
where my passions still flourish
in the night of the luminous moon.

In the twilight of earliest morning
the wind is starting to sing;
the softened whistling of flautists
floats through the air of the dawn.

Out of the shadows now surges
the withered fortress of stone,
where the rosebush still diffuses

the scent of an enchanted past,
where a princess in timeless slumber
awaits me to rekindle her breath.

CXXV

Mythical creatures like the Centaur Chion,
the gentle, loved by virgins, unicorn;
or Medusa, whose gaze could turn a man to stone,
the three-headed, fire-breathing chimera... are

metaphorical expressions of human ideals,
are in perpetual haunting motion
to project immemorial sensations,
of bathing in balmy Elysian sunshine

or aching in chilly chthonian chasms
clamouring the divine tone of the Orphean harp,
that once enchanted the goddess Athena,

who in her night-wandering chariot
with the moonlight glinting off her armour
tried to rescue Orpheus, clasping her

Gorgon-headed, snake-fringed aegis.

CXXVI

The enamoured stranger
whom no one could name
ignored all danger
enhancing his fame.

In the light of the moon,
the sirens, alluring and bare,
would the mariner maroon
with their sensual snare.

The nameless phantom
duped the treacherous sea,
but was unable to fathom

that on Tauris' shore he could be,
where he reached his final abyss
sacrificed to Artemis.

CXXVII

On the shore of the island Patmos,
the obsessively periphrastic venture
into bold Homeric archaism – with
the sun descending over and over;

a magnificent pitch of intensity
teeters over the Aegean Sea,
a perfect moulding of tone,
phrasing of thesis, and theme,

never out of balance,
pathos, and passion,
eternal as air and water,

the high and the profound,
sea sirens singing to me
on the dancing starlit waves.

CXXVIII

Il voyageait dans les vallées de la Panonie.
Sa lyre résonnait dans les montagnes d'Ismaros,
la rivière Hebrus réfléchissait sa mélancolie.
En la lointaine Trace il trouve sa fin atroce.

Dieux et mortels et les non-vivants
étaient séduits par ses chants poignants.
Toutes les Ménards étaient amoureuses de lui;
sa voix les transportait en extases la nuit.

Ces femmes orgiaques qui mangent les lauriers,
le malheureux, brutalement et avec pathos,
dans leur dépravations l'ont déchiré.

Ou vengèrent-ils la fureur de Dionysos
pour célébrer le lever du soleil sur le Mont Pangaion
chaque matin honorant Phébus à l'horizon?

CXXIX *An English Version*

He journeyed through the valleys of Pannonia.
His lyre echoed in the hills of Ismaros,
and the river Hebrus mirrored his *malincolia*;
his death in Thrace was barbarous!

Gods and mortals and the unliving
were enthralled by his poignant chants.
The maenads, aroused by his virile singing,
were thrown into an orgiastic trance.

These wild, laurel-chewing women
tore the peripatetic minstrel apart,
in a frenzy forever unforgiven,

or for neglecting Dionysus' art,
since Phoebus he honoured on the horizon
cheering the sunrise in the hilly environ.

CXXX

His choice was absolute and tragic,
reflected in the choric songs of converts,
stirring the throng with intense emotion,
with passion captured the ears of man.

Hidden under mounds of earth,
the lucid flicker of a soulful life,
a scattered dialogue of self and gods,
his name will live in song and odes.

Like the sun he glistened in his ardour
and chose his death to live forever,
transforming into a glittering star.

The resounding tone of his *kithara*
which ardently sings to our blood
echoes passionately into the night.

CXXXI

I am evermore convinced
that love is just imagination,
that invents the glowing sunsets
and the flowering *primavera,*

that dreams up magic summer nights
and the entrancing *piena luna,*
an alluring *ninfa* dancing
on the waves of pristine streams,

and your divinely-shaped contours,
your bewitching, beaming eyes,
that it imagines you and me,

Orpheus, singing Apollonian airs
enchanting graceful *naïades*
and birds and ageless stone.

CXXXII

I would travel to my homeland again,
beyond mountains and perilous terrain,
but all my people were slain in the war,
in *Thrace* no one knows me anymore.

Soon, too soon, will be approaching the time,
my song will no longer with nightingale rhyme.
I will be taken to a tenebrous sphere
and soon be forgotten even out here.

Maybe Calliope will sing my dirge
sounding a brooding meditation on love,
but not even a skillful thaumaturge,

could save me, nor Olympian gods above.
Thanatos, an avatar of Achilles,
made his deadly diagnosis.

CXXXIII

He said his name was Sandagupta,
(but *Indoi* sounded more melodious)
insisting that he was a *brämacäria,*
son of a *bräman,* learning the scripts.

Freed slave of my friend Filoraios,
who acquired the boy in Mitanni
from a merchant of far Nineveh
who had brought him, fettered, from Elam.

Esoteric verses soon clung to his lyre;
he sang of self and endless cosmos
endowed with atman, with life and fire,

with Brahma, the very breath and thought,
the enlightenment of mortal man, sang
of samsara, karma, of the god Vishnu,

with rapture and awe uttered… nirvana.

CXXXIV

Lift your lyre and start to play,
and let wine yield holy shivers,
let rapture reign another day,
before you cross perilous rivers.

Muses and nymphs, the sky
grapevines and flower seeds,
the ripening days now vie
with old heroic deeds.

The obliteration of Troy –
scarce memories of joy!
But to Ithaca's king has sung

Eumaeus the swineherd
that *fortuna* has swung.
Challenge the tempests undeterred!

CXXXV

El verano ya termina,
hojas caen lentamente,
y el viento adivina
la frescura claramente.

El sol ya se debilita,
y las flores se lamentan.
La alegría se agota,
cuando las rosas se acuestan.

Murmullos ya del invierno
en lo profundo de mi alma!
Toco un acorde tierno

que en la noche da la calma.
Siempre suena nuestra canción
en mi agradecido corazón.

CXXXVI An English Version

The summer has now ended;
the leaves are slowly falling.
Long shadows are now calling;
chill and bleakness have descended.

The sun has lost its healing power,
luminosity is fading,
resignation is prevailing,
ever slowly turns the hour.

Winter murmurs fill the air;
in the deep space of my heart
sounds a well-loved melody,

that long ago we used to share,
and still lives on in nature's art,
rings inside me most fervently.

CXXXVII

The echoes of my dream awaken
the morning twilight of Argolis
still breathing the cold mountain air
of the unfathomable night.

The Isthmus' shadows loom in silence
and soundless is my anguished heart,
but blossoms from the olive grove
engulf me with their redolence.

And the evening glow soon stirs
new hope in songless days
in quest of sublime revelations,

for, deprived of the resplendent sun,
I resume my trying search
by the dim light of the stars.

CXXXVIII

The fortifications of Aeropolis,
where hundreds of faces would pale,
awaited the onslaught of foes
resulting from rhetorical slights.

The Furies of Hades rejoiced
at the sight of the river of blood,
like red dye scattered over the waves
at the threshold of chthonian doom.

The characteristic interpolation,
the allegorical and the confirmed
with manic examples of gloom

plunged into the deep Plutonian night,
with sunbeams buried under red clay,
in a nefarious, invisible world.

CXXXIX

Un velo cubre la circumstancia,
ese talento del espíritu
lo miraban con devoción
en la noche del poeta.

Premoniciones en sus versos,
un rayo de luna en el agua,
noche de fiesta y de júbilo
sobre el mar jovial.

Un tono nuevo y alto
ha levantado mil velas
esta noche estrellada.

Un encantamiento con agua y luna
extático bailar de las ninfas,
himnos a la diosa de la tierra.

CXL An English Version

A subtle veil capped the event;
this talented spiritual rhymer
they looked upon with fervour
in the bright night of the poet.

Premonitions in his verses,
rays of moonlight over the water,
night of sensation and joy,
jubilant soaring over the sea.

A tone, unique and steep
has raised a thousand sails
on this clear and starry night.

An intoxication with water and moon,
ecstatic dancing of nymphs on the waves,
singing hymns to the goddess of Earth.

CXLI

Knowledge kept in hermetic circles
lit by the flame of rapt *poiesis,*
a true exchange of cerebral waves
in stone enclosure of deep thought.

But looking at the setting sun,
in the land of ancient myths
fell a huge deluge of grief
on luminous primeval glyphs.

On Aegean shores the song resounded
in lengthy trills of lamentation
when Scythian wolves devoured light,

when strong Herakles suffered pain,
embraced a monstrous rock in vain
to pluck the entrance to Hades.

CXLII

Moonlight towering overhead
with an acute artistic vision,
a rare musical topography
takes on a sense of homogeneity.

Lengthy thoughts and prodigious vigils,
are delicate meditations on the world,
but also luxuriant, exciting, and bold,
as a midnight ode hails the starry mould.

The shepherds on Mount Cithaeron hear
Orpheus in a cathartic appearance
in sublime triumph over the occurrence,

as the star of morning rises
to paraphrase with fervent glee
its glinting image on the sea.

CXLIII

My ardent songs go fly to her,
messengers of my yearnings be,
my rapture and resolve confer.
Soar across the Aegean Sea!

Loyal lyre, send my love,
from my heart a melody.
To grace my dreams is not enough;
tell her of my ecstasy!

And let Aeolus stir the wind
to sing my verses in her ear,
that I would nevermore rescind

to join her on the highest sphere,
that in ethereal felicity
we dream beyond eternity.

CXLIV

I am a stranger in this land;
familiar sights have disappeared.
Trees and stones that one time cheered,
my songs no longer understand.

Who now weaves my destiny?
The wind has blown my hat away;
where are the kindly faces, say!
Neither man nor beast remembers me.

There is nothing left that waits out here;
take me then to Hades' walls,
to the gloomy world of shades.

Gods of darkness can you hear?
Let me inside your ghostly halls
to join my erstwhile jovial mates!

CXLV

En la noche fresca y serena,
sobre una alfombra muda
que me aclara ciertas palabras,
tomo el camino del exilio.

Retornaré un día no lejano
adonde mi inocencia vive aún,
vive el clarín del ruiseñor,
viven hadas silenciosas.

Trás una tapia de piedra,
adonde está mi secreto entraré,
donde mi pasión vive aún.

Superando todo obstáculo,
a la ciudadela de Mycenae
accederé sin hacer ruido.

CXLVI An English Version

The night, uncloudy and cool,
stretching over the silent plain,
resolving a few arduous thoughts,
drives me onto my exile road,

but one day, I know, I will return,
where my innocence still lives,
where legendary spirits loom,
and a nightingale my verses sings.

From behind the wall of stone
will I enter where my secret lives on,
where my passion still stirs.

Overwhelming all hurdles and hitches,
the slumbering citadel of Mycenae
I will enter in utter silence.

CXLVII

Flashes of lightning,
ephemeral magicians,
keep the masked dancers
in concentric circles,

and bless all
who breathe
a god's fire
that flares and sings

immemorial hymns
simple and holy
in its upward spiral;

a magic apparition
with animistic sparkle
jolts the god-fearing throng.

CXLVIII

The astonished believers,
on the Tempe's shore,
fixate the abstruse cyphers
of their wilted lore

floating on the rushing stream,
those who build their temple
on the arduous slope
of the worship of blood.

The murderous knife
slips into the agora
to embrace the archimage,

who is no doubt the curse
and the double game
of an enamoured soul.

CXLIX

Like the endless beat of time,
you, proud and noble river pass,
hail the sunrise splendid climb
and flow with grace and *gravitas;*

pursue your course as if in flight,
and steer your winding escapades
through fields and meadows with delight.
Evenings, you clasp dimming shades,

but in the morning bathe in light.
In the throe of a primeval rite,
Scythian gods slid on your snares.

With your current they then sailed,
Achaeans, singing enraptured airs,
who from far horizons hailed.

CL

I wandered through her holy grove,
where Artemis turned Actaeon
into a stag to hunt him down,
when he watched her virgins bathe.

I had closed my eyes in blind affection,
when I thought I heard the shrieks
of frenzied Furies in broad *fugato*,
as spades of iron in *unisono*

struck my head *fortissimo*
in fragmentary and strident tone,
when horns and drums resumed the theme,

and Thanatos' cohorts tried to drag me
to the threshold of my darkest dream,
but the huntress' certain arrows

saved me once more from Hades' hosts.

CLI

A sweeping passacaglia,
a rhapsodic, swaying melody,
in fragmentary Phrygia
a majestic, moving threnody.

To reach remote peripheries,
a vision of harmonic dice,
a motto runs through all the keys
as idiomorphic sacrifice.

When a deceitful serpent's sting
let her languish in Hades' caves,
I let my loyal lyre sing,

an ardent melody extol,
to stir the ghostly river's waves,
the arrival of my shade to toll.

CLII

Freedom devoid of ethical proportions,
meaning from meaningless expression
extracted from the tragedy, to moralize
the harsh note of human sacrifice.

The Heracleidae find refuge in Athens
contradicting surface tensions;
like arrows along the river's shore,
the metaphor is striking.

Bound for the sky or Tartarus,
the surrender to an ethereal state,
a shadow image of our world,

with links as far as Lake Averno
or beyond the pillars of Herakles,
escaping into twilit bondage.

CLIII

Über die höchsten Wolken schwebend,
über uns unbekannten Ländern,
die geheimnisvollen Fluren des Himmels
entfalten sich über den Horizont hinaus.

Süßer Traum einer vergessenen Nacht
strecke deine verschundenen Flügel aus,
komm zurück aus Arkadiens Feldern
und steige aus deinem Gedächtnis heraus.

Wie das Echo eines Wiegenliedes,
gesungen von der Göttin Gaia
das die ganze Erde berührt,

eure Melodie der Abendruhe,
Sirenen der rauschenden Meere
zieht Schiffer in die träumerische Leere.

CLIV An English Version

Floating over highest clouds,
over lands to us unknown,
the enigmatic fields of heaven
unfurl beyond the far horizon.

Sweet dream of a forgotten night,
extend your vanished pinions;
return from Arcadia's flowering fields,
and surface from your memory.

Like the echo of a cradle song,
sung by the goddess Gaia,
which touches everything on Earth,

you alluring, tempting sirens,
divas of the roaring seas,
sing sleep-inducing melodies.

CLV

They had honoured us with crowns of ivy,
when in the shade of an olive grove
by the shore of the Ionian Sea,
we breathed Elysian air,

where delightful Aphrodite
covered us with vernal bloom,
as my exalted lyre
resounded with pastoral tunes.

I hummed an ardent Achaean refrain
while drinking spirited wine,
and you, happy as the orioles

whistling in the flowering trees,
sang my glowing verses
into the Aegean sunset.

CLVI

A gush of springtime airiness,
delightful twitter in the trees
and a flowering elevation
suffuses him with exaltation.

In his labyrinth of verses,
multiple strains of divination,
since language cast in sortilege,
blossom raptly in his mind,

and unrestrained by silken leaches,
they will not grasp his intimation
of honouring chthonian gods,

his peculiar transformation
of gliding on the scheming Styx
attracting shadows to his myth.

CLVII

Melodious wind,
a starlit night,
divine imprint
of life's delight.

Your blissful smile,
rose lustrous light,
in my exile
a transcendent might.

Now I will live,
starry-eyed,
prone to relive

the magic night
in Thracian hills –
if a goddess wills.

CLVIII

What joy of life around me blooming,
a tranquil stream through golden fields;
the glowing sun-god dips his horses
into the cooling Aegean Sea!

Flowers in meadows, beasts in forests,
listen to my exalted harp,
and eagles soar to lofty peaks
heralding my lyrics to the sky!

How music rings in many colours
in the twilit rolling soundscape,
Muses exalt the evening splendour!

Archaic Dorian melodies
are flaming on the rapt horizon
like roses lit by an elated sun!

CLIX

… and fervidly yearn the flowers
for the splendour of the waves.
Their lilac and purple shades
bereft of light like in a prison

in the evening of gloom by the sea,
where his song of lamentation,
in a poignant presentation,
the intonation is exceedingly clear.

His lyre's natural resonance
in a rare musical depth
is punctuated with wildfire fury,

his wayward trajectory reflecting
the garlands of roses and meliots
he once flung into the fiery flood.

CLX

Tenebrous space, impervious to time,
sustains the ever-expanding *kosmos,*
where fiery Hades emits a potent spark
for us mortals to thrive in the shade.

The ecstatic, ever-enriching spirit,
graced with the music of the spheres
and invigorated with Aegean wine,
is greater in a flash of time

than an eternity of sober thought.
Still looking for the gods in glittering stars?
Better to rest under a flowering tree,

at midday, by a cooling source,
follow the brooklet to the river of dreams –
coursing into the deep waters of bliss.

CLXI

Cuando los dioses huyeron,
de las colinas elocuentes de Beocia,
de sus rios intentaba aprender
y de las tardes solemnes

que pasaba en las arboledas
abajo del cielo locuaz del crepúsculo.
El encanto de la naturaleza,
su ámbito celeste,

me condujo hacia el Helespunto
donde los espíritus de heroes
me hicieron cantar sus odas

y mi lira pintaba frescos,
alegría apolínea,
en las murallas míticas de Troya.

CLXII An English Version

When the gods fled from us,
from Boeotia's eloquent hills
and rivers I tried to learn,
and from the solemn evenings

I spent in Argolisian olive groves
under a twilit loquacious sky.
The spell of nature's phenomena
imbued with divine devotion,

led me to the Hellespont,
where the spirits of storied heroes
made me sing the odes of old,

and my lyre painted frescos,
radiant Apollonian joy
on the mythical walls of Troy.

CLXIII

He made a fateful acquaintance
with deep and prodigious mystique,
a chthonian world covered with garlands
and labyrinths of Achaean verse

exalting tragic chivalry
blossoming like an Aegean myth,
a yearning for a bygone age,
an Achillean thirst for death and glory,

but the superlative lyric hero
noted for his words, not war,
like the rustle of autumn leaves

with a muted sweep of rhythm,
in the spell of syllables
of panegyrical stanzas – sang

paeans to the god Apollo!

CLXIV

Ancient twilights are still trying
to enhance the Earth's unstoppable dying.
Questions blossom, concealing broadening strife
in the glimmer of vernal stirrings of life.

Odysseus meets the shade of Achilles
who tells him to dream and from conflict refrain,
since battles won are all but in vain,
bitten by a snake was strong Herakles.

But under glistening pebbles concealed
remain slivers of hope for relevant verse,
songs to console the suffering Earth.

Flaming Apollo must his fire wield,
or else I will close my tormented eyes
and wait for another sun to arise.

CLXV

Eastward from Delphi,
Cadmus, son of Argiope,
who slew the vile serpent
and built our citadel, despaired

when even the blind seer,
Tiresias, spurred
to wear the skin of fauns
and went to Cithaeron

to greet Dionysus,
the youngest of the gods,
whose sojourn in auriferous

Phrygia had been glorious
and triumphant his visit
to mountainous Thrace.

CLXVI

How fair is untamed Cithaeron,
lush and green her scented glades,
fountains clear as crystal flow
out of pristine, rocky caves!

The sound of a distant *dithyrambos* –
an alluring voice now beckons all
to the land of prodigious joy
where Dionysus appears.

Rejoice and dance, O Boeotia,
chant the frantic bassarids,
welcome the son of Semele

and god of gods, All-Father Zeus!
By her grave, I watch the flame
flare in fervent veneration –

and heed the call to Cithaeron.

CLXVII

He spent his time roaming
calmly over barren land,
over stormy seas,
and mountain peaks,

far from the flower gardens.
Whirlwinds in open spaces
and *dies irae* in the temple
do not mask the chorus

of orphic devotees
with monolithic eyes
immersed in rites of purification,

participating in the great secret
of the exultant god, Dionysus,
revelling in his mysteries.

CLXVIII

Joy is sometimes surreptitious
and often stirs after a storm.
Although the rainbow disappears,
it leaves behind a pleasing glow.

A feeling of lightheartedness
between contentment and pure bliss
is what propels us mortals
to clamber silken cliffs,

raising eyes when left below
or looking down from mountain peaks
in search of grace and splendour,

the crimson of the setting sun
over gleaming seas
and roseate twitter in the trees!

CLXIX

Another singular occurrence
of my many vexations:
beyond the shores of Attica
my lyre dared the tempest.

Languishing vapours
disparaged the sunrise,
while Achelous' daughters
sang enticing airs.

I was lost at sea,
saw dusky ravens,
headless, riding the waves

and grey wolves
of colossal strength
in the shreds of the twilight.

CLXX

He prayed to Father Zeus for guidance
and called to his mother, Semele,
to leave the realm of the dead
when he bathed in Aegean sunshine

surrounded by the ruins of Thebes,
the Bassarids and Maenades
leading a long procession,
as their dithyrambic hymns

merged with euphoric cries
to Dionysus, the ecstatic god,
the conquering hero of the Aegean world,

who stood by the grave of Semele
and relighted the sacred flame
that Penteus, the new king of Thebes,

had spitefully extinguished.

CLXXI

Some flowers don't grow from the earth,
yet enchant my senses with prodigious joy.
Aphrodite, ever young and radiant,
whose divine pulchritude

I exalt in my paeans and hymns
in rapt and elevated tone – while
the exuberant sun of the days of Eurydice
rings a golden note in the distance,

where bees still dance with butterflies,
but the call of larks is forever lost.
My thoughts and emotions soar upward

and linger beneath the high dome of time
shadowing the temple of the goddess of love,
where the spirits of heroines are kept safe.

CLXXII

Springtime *melos* embraces me,
a breath of wonder everywhere;
my heart is filled with florid glee
and swelled with song and vernal air.

I want to climb the highest mountain
to better scan Earth's paradise,
drink the nectar of its fountain
that in dreams of rapture lies.

Overwhelmed with magic bloom,
kneeling, spreading out my arms,
let homage to the heavens zoom,

and transported by a goddess' charms,
let my elated lyre soar,
enamoured sing her timeless lore.

CLXXIII

He proceeded from Thebes' ruins
gleaming in the sublime vespertine sun
connecting the near and far
in complex syntax and theme

while they looked for proof of aberration
in his greatly eccentric verse
written in sibyllic tone
praising the ever-young Aphrodite

wearing a tight *cantabile* dress
who in her divine beauty
in his mythical plan

enticed Apollo to strike
formidable Python with his bow
to avenge Eurydice's woeful death.

CLXXIV

Una vez, cerca de la salida del sol
escuchaba, y contento te esperaba en la colina.
Mi paciencia era reconpensada
cuando oía las hojas susurrar,

y tu apareciste de la niebla
del averno despertando,
de las islas oscuras
del río olvidadizo, del Leteo,

con ojos de asombro
en esos días hermosos
cuando aprendía

de las estrellas
que encantaban
los campos vastos de mis sueños.

CLXXV An English Version

Once, in the morning twilight,
I waited for you in the hills
with my heart surging
when I heard the rustle of leaves,

and you emerged from the haze
of the awakening world below,
from the forgotten myths
of the river Lethe

with eyes of wonder,
in those days of beauty
when I was overwhelmed

with sublime stirrings
of enchantment
in the pastures of my dreams.

CLXXVI

Now I sit silent and intrigued
and gaze beyond the azure sky,
beyond joy and grief
into the twilight of my fate.

I would still sing with the stars
waiting for a resplendent spring,
the greening of the breeze
emanating from Boeotia,

for an intense absorption
enraptures my senses
and elates the rock of my solitude

overhanging the gleaming waters
of an enchanted Aegean Sea,
pulsing its primordial songs.

CLXXVII

Après les prés d'Arcadie en fleurs
aux ombres chtoniennes inquiétantes,
les flûtes pastorales des songeurs
remplacées par les Furies irritantes.

Tu te souviens, Eurydice,
nos rêves élyséens
sur la tour élancée de Mycènes,
le bonheur des vivantes de jadis!

Mais ton retour, tu célébras,
un magnifique événement;
du sommet, tu regarderas

les champs d'Argolis allégrement.
Trouve ton haleine encore une fois;
mes chansons, au soleil les envoie!

CLXXVIII An English Version

From blooming Arcadian meadows
into cheerless chthonian shades,
dreamy pastoral flutes
making way to screaming Furies!

Do you remember, Eurydice,
our Elysian musings
on the soaring tower of Mycenae,
the ethereal joy of the living?

But your return shall be celebrated,
a great and wonderful event,
looking down from the summit

onto the pastures of placid Argolis,
once more finding your breath
and singing my songs to the sun.

CLXXIX

On that torrid midsummer day,
I saw your glistening flourishing hair
swaying in the breeze,
your eyes, sparkling with emotion,

saw me linger by the shore,
and your smile, in blinding glitter,
was echoing the beaming sun.
Holding onto a leafless tree,

I watched you plunge, enticing and bare,
into the wild and hurried waters
of the cascading pristine stream,

singing in stinging *fioritura*,
the moment moulding into stone,
a monument to rapt illusion.

CLXXX

Ask among gods and heroes!
The dead are ferried over the Styx,
an epic in decasyllable couplets
chanted to the deep tone of the *kithara*.

But the question remains otiose;
his deeds assure him immortality,
with the Muses singing his glory,
Naïades dressing his corpse in robes of beauty.

Amid epigrams and apophthegms
and supersensory intuition,
his passion for Aegean *melos*

sails beyond earthly dimensions
to settle on the mystic shore,
the cult centre of the *kyrios*

of the *kosmos*.

CLXXXI *Primavera*

How long have I been dreaming
in a deep and dusky maze,
of your trees and azure ceiling,
of birds and song and flowering days?

You manifest your splendour
in sparkle and array,
make melancholy surrender
in your rapt and stunning way,

make kindly spirits rise again
from pristine source and meadow,
surround me with your sweet refrain,

free me of Hades' shadow,
and grant my lyre eagle wings
that your song above Parnassus rings.

CLXXXII Achaean Poet

Born out of history and fantasy,
the evocative and emotive nature,
the magnificence of the god-king,
spread a vital reflection of light

with the elegance of a passacaglia
in a stream of musical transport,
the god's otherworldly glitter
a torrent of cosmic flare.

Not even the greatest of the *tholoi,*
the vaulted tombs of Mycenae,
could embrace the wondrous king

whose eternal luminescence
enthralls an awed Achaean ποιητής
looking up to the nightly Aegean sky.

CLXXXIII

The great enigma that lies in wait,
choosing the timorous inaudible rose,
or diligent bees that buzz in the field,
the hazy edges of a mysterious world!

Poets, like falcons, are required to soar,
can allude to but cannot express
the primordial bottomless night
sounding her strident thunderous soul.

Images worn away by the ages,
legends and deeds in silent embrace,
wilted wisdom chiselled in stone,

but the search to connect with immortals
savours the splendour of holy design,
the hieroglyphical syntax of life.

CLXXXIV

Worshipping Demeter in her temple
to spur the growth on buoyant earth,
to her laws be deferential
that Eleusis thrive in wealth and births!

Her feast in Thesmophoria
where songs in elevated tone,
his paeans stir euphoria,
move birds and mortals, trees and stone!

And the glowing disk up high
exhibits brilliance and joy,
makes Persephone and Hades sigh,

alights old memories of Troy
where shades of daring heroes roam,
Demeter's Eleusinian mysteries loom.

CLXXXV

My ship embellished with garlands
sailing over the Aegean Sea,
in its sunlit endeavour transcends
all in the *kosmos,* exalted and free.

I hail the glow of the autumn sky
and the long-awaited harvest,
sun-coloured fruits from Boeotia vie
with the *melos* of the fluting artist

to celebrate my Aegean dreams
on the altar of flowering airs,
an adventure with ethereal themes,

where the song of my offering flares
over the cliffs of lofty Mount Athos,
soars with fervour, passion, and pathos.

CLXXXVI

The gods' all-assuming presence
in the wind-swept valley of light
in diverse voices and tones,
a dazzling, glimmering sky

in the rapt Aegean sunset;
almond-blossom-like redolence
denoting phonic syllables,
in a breeze of secret chants

express the pulses of artistic perception,
the poetic persona in search of
the faint trace of earliest Athenians,

the destiny of prodigious times,
beyond reason and explanation
ambushed in poisonous glitter

resounding in purest musical tone.

CLXXXVII

Shadowing the seaboards of fabled Argolis,
the dreamlike poignant yearnings
on the vast slope of a mysterious mount
lingering in primordial array,

and from behind the myths and masks
looking at the sunset from the summit,
onto the fiery, floriferous verve
breathing the scent of magical days,

arming poets with weapons of wonder,
and filling their eyes with hallowed display
on the felicitous shores of Aegean lands

when impassioned gods throw open the gate,
turning the autumn into a golden adventure,
as the sea roars onto the strands of the Isthmus!

CLXXXVIII

He shattered musical boundaries!
Explorations of spatial dimensions
bridging the earthly and the divine,
sharing the clarity of moon and stars,

a super conception of light and beyond;
the effect of song on flower and stone
taking flight in his imagination
in quest of the ultimate, the Elysian tone!

Orpheus, crushed by the loss of his nymph,
asks if the sun also shines for the dead,
according with the musical and the immortal,

but a great mystery lies darkly in wait
beyond the unconquered mountains of mind,
in the boundless emptiness

of visionary shadows.

CLXXXIX

Flowers and the singing of birds make me sad
when rain fills the wind in the darkened sky
rigorously with every musical metre,
in an array of austere, ritualized styles,

yielding languishing combinations
of timbre, colour, and pulse –
yet every day I go out searching
to reunite with your spirit, Eurydice.

Aleatorically and intuitively,
you extend my fervour
when the day shines golden,

when you gather melodious bloom
in the redolent Elysian Fields –
my lyre strumming wistful refrains.

CXC

El fuego que abrasa mi vida
en el recuerdo o en la imaginación
me ha del todo revelado
el misterio oculto en el fragor

del rio turbulento de la voluntad
cayendo en un vértigo sin fondo
en un rincón ignoto de la tierra
del que óndas han surgido con

una canción maravillosamente
rebosada de mi copa llena de vino
que me aclara ciertas palabras

escritos en las vides florecientes
agitadas por el viento suave del sur
más puro que la lírica impetuosa

de las olas del Mar Jonico.

CXCI An English Version

The fire that enflames my life
in memory or in imagination
has fully enlightened me
as to the mystery hidden in the sound

of the turbulent willful stream
cascading vertically into the void
at an unknown corner of the world
from whose soundwaves has marvellously

surged a long-forgotten song spilling
over the rim of my wine-filled cup
explaining the meaning of words

written on the flourishing vines
swayed by a melodious breeze
purer than the raving chants

of the waves of the Ionian Sea.

CXCII

He sang an archaic Dorian refrain
in the temple devoted to Theseus,
artfully blending various colours
and images simple and holy.

The magical power of music
released its churning emotion,
diffusing joy and elation
with virtuosity and flair,

and from Parnassus re-emerged
a rich and sustained celestial tone
like time measured by the flow of waves

of Ulysses' violet-hued sea
or the rhythmic trickle of sand –
just a note in Chronos' timeless refrain.

CXCIII

Artemis snatched Iphigenia away from death,
leaving instead a hind to be killed
when the virgin turned pale in her mortal distress;
the forces of darkness were once more repelled.

Where the omens say the maiden went,
to the distant shores of mythical Tauris,
the unfolding of an enormous event
sung by her ever shadowing chorus,

as seen in an image wilted by time
to mask the bright and golden shade
and its style, metre, and rhyme,

thus, chronological order may well be lost,
time frames confounded by unyielding fate
of an intriguing and fleeting past.

CXCIV

In a stream of musical transport
it surges like a pristine fount
and glitters like desert sand in the sun
with dynamic contrasts chosen at will

that guide its rapt melancholic songs
which soar to an amazing and massive close
while murmurs from an earlier age
spread a faint reflection of light

down to the abysses of doubt and despair
with a sudden flourish of verse
that the notion of *ever* persists

as a portrayal of cosmic rebirth
letting the dramatic power of fate
flow over the dark blossoms of earth.

CXCV

An intense meditation on life
in perilous mountainous terrain
or in oracular temples of Boeotia,
in the labyrinth of a flowering mind.

Swayed gently by the breath of *Zephyros,*
earth blossoms in divine splendour
permeate the placid vespertine airs
like opiate chants of a bygone age.

But storm clouds obscure the horizon,
and the night's dusky roses
I cannot braid into her hair.

The anguish of separation looms;
Ilium and the Hellespont
call with compelling persistence.

CXCVI

Praising the splendour of his vision,
his glowing aspect of imagination
in the fountainhead of *son et lumière*
pulsing with fervent reverberation!

The fire of his mystical flare,
the intensity of his resonant verse,
conceived in the heat of Ilium's war,
exalting the undaunted, flowering Earth,

the tempting blossoming flora
in the meadows of vernal Argolis
rousing goats or enamoured satyrs!

Pan's flautists' rapt magic display,
the Attic genius' noblest inebriation
inscribed at Pylus on tablets of clay!

CXCVII

The splendid full moon,
brilliant and fair,
a nymph, alluring and bare,
a night in redolent June,

as my lyre's delirious tune
enchanted the vernal air,
and the moon's luminous glare
bedazzled the glittering dune.

Fairer than a flowering iris,
she stood before me in full view.
I sang to her, in rapture and awe,

an otherworldly bliss,
a goddess, are you,
a wonder of legend and lore.

CXCVIII

Trailing Homer's heroic myths
is glimpsing tenebrous Hades
since death is ever victorious,
Ares' cruelest claim.

Atreus' sons laid siege to Troy,
Achilles, in a flaring, manic rage,
spurred to avenge Patroclus;
killing the hero Hector and twelve

Trojan youths on the pyre of his friend –
but Ilium's tale lives ever on
written with blood on glittering bone,

and the sirens' songs of fate
blow through the cavities of stone
in rapt and terrifying tone.

CXCIX

A gentle breeze of secret chants
blossoms in a sublime world;
the whispers of my lyre's strings
hail from a wondrous gleaming sphere.

From Parnassus looms another dream;
shades inflame the mountain air
like riddles drifting to the shore,
in the colours of the sinking sun.

My tortured syntax to abandon,
hymns and fragments of my hymns
chose the boldest forms of death.

But let me live just one more spring
of rapt, transcendent, aurous tone,
once more with the Muses sing,

again, bedazzle flower and stone!

CC

Am Abend erreichte ich den alten Hafen
als über den See die Sonne sank,
dachte nicht ans Ruhen und Schlafen
der Blume in deinen Haaren dank.

Das Wasser spiegelte der Sonne Blüten
wie das Lächeln um deinen Rosenmund,
und Töne aus deiner *kithara* sprühten
Achäische Klänge von Stund zu Stund.

Ich war versunken im Zauber der Feier.
Du sangest die Lieder von deinem Heimatland,
und aus deinen Augen das jugendliche Feuer

brachte mich zwingend um meinen Verstand –
Oft lausch ich der *kithara* bei sinkender Sonne
und vergeh noch immer in glühender Wonne.

CCI An English Version

At the old haven I looked for repose,
in the evening when the unruffled sea
gleamed like a splendid red-tinged rose,
as the sun sank with grace and esprit,

but I was hardly aware of nature's spell,
saw only the flower adorning your hair,
and your smile would vanquish my will
when you plucked chords with passion and flair.

Your *kithara* rang like an Apollonian lyre,
and your song engulfed me like a flowering wave,
your eyes, glowing with youthful fire,

turned me into their compliant slave –
I still hear the echoes of your poignant chants
when the red-hued sun sets in Aegean lands.

CCII

The shady linden trees as ever
shed their motley autumn leaves,
with primordial endeavour
stir perennial beliefs,

fill the lonely wanderer's prayer
with wilted and with wistful thoughts
of his goddess called *Antheia*
and her *fioritura* modes.

Wherever she now loves and dreams
the world around her glints and gleams.
I know, I know, the autumn trees

bedazzle me with sad allure –
but will she in a tuneful breeze
her voice for me once more conjure?

CCIII

The fig tree captures the lingering wind,
the musical dice game commences
the metaphysical and mythical search
at the outer limits of an enigmatic world.

Behind the innocent and the stridently new,
the deepest veracity of our time,
the *aletheia* wearing an Achaean disguise
with a tinge of death in her dazzling design.

The final trust of her zealous sword –
by a stroke of her timely celestial spell,
the heavens cast off their iron fence.

The shimmering valley exposes the summer,
but the majestic gods in massive marble
claim for themselves the principal themes!

CCIV

I see the eternal in the light of the sunset,
and the sonically adventurous part of the sky
break through the gates of deepest perception,
the musical expansion at the most concerted

when the night is lurking behind the cypresses,
the moonbeams transforming into celestial chords
and my ship in the twilight sailing over the sea,
blue like an extension of the heavenly vault.

Euphonic extremes at the most rhapsodic,
the coming together of flower and stone,
the breathtaking ideal of a vital spark!

But could my life be dreamlike, inane to the gods,
only a drop in the temporal ocean,
the truth of my being just a loan of the mind?

CCV

The sparkling lucidities of interior life,
a spirited dialogue of self and soul,
a remoteness felt in time and space,
as the day of death is closing in.

In the grip of a Dionysian paroxysm,
forceful, daemonic, and unfathomable,
the pathos of wishing annihilation
echoes with infinite variations.

In the Lethe's waters will I bathe;
yearning is singing through my blood.
We Achaeans muse in epigrams!

Invisible verse forms like *isopsephia;*
time has set off as sacred ground
in the gentle blue of far horizons.

CCVI

Más allá de las arcadas de piedra
para celebrar la buena nueva;
allí en la época primaveral
reforzando el mito evocador

en busca de enigmas singulares,
asistir en el sueño completo
a punto de romperse hermosamente
en las sombras, ondas, y montañas,

donde en las cumbres maravillosas,
se hubo puesto a soplar el viento
en esta tiniebla mística.

En la luz tenue del laberinto,
donde estaba mi destino, relucía
vestido por mi última hazaña.

CCVII An English Version

Beyond the withered arcades of stone
when the first spring blossoms gleamed
to celebrate the joyful occasion,
diffused by an evocative myth

in quest of enigmatic exploits,
reinforced by a singular dream
at the point of an exquisite demise
in shades, soundwaves, and mountains,

in whose majestic culminations
the wind had started to stir
in a rapturous twilit sweep,

there, in the dim light of the labyrinth,
where my destiny had taken me,
I glistened, dressed for my final adventure.

CCVIII

When my long wanderings
have finally ended
and the Muses sing my hymns,
will my spirit then live?

Will I live in the melody
of the late autumn breeze?
Will I live?
Will I live in languishing airs?

The wind that shakes the branches
of the leafless, shivering tree,
will it lament?

Will it lament my inglorious death?
Will it bewail
the death of my songs?

CCIX

They had conceived a noble feast,
an ecstatic poetic presentation
like their forebears after heroic deeds,
a keen *desideratum* of the heart

by the orphic throng that gathered
in the sacred hills beyond the Hebrus,
where the superlative minstrel,
priest of much maligned Dionysus,

obtained a glorious apotheosis,
was acclaimed a god more hallowed
than the gatherer of motely clouds…

The marching white-roped acolytes
halted, raised their arms toward the sky,
asking to be purified, be worthy of

a blissful, harmonious tone –
of Orpheus' eternal harp.

CCX

Where the lily grows wild in the valley,
Orpheus sings of love and wine,
exalts the flowering primavera
where the robins tweet Athena went,

where the fate of prodigious aeons,
filled with movement and adventure,
leaves behind a golden shadow
in the pristine mirror of a dream.

The heavenly fire cannot be quenched;
by way of the pure word
il fuoco viene addosso a noi.

The poet exposes the gods' glitter;
pulsing with hallowed introspection,
his hymns echoing from heaven's vault.

the fire comes down on us.

CCXI

Enterpe, in my bitter torments,
will you give my heart new hope,
fashion that my sorrow ends,
make me with my fervour cope?

How poor those mortals who could never
know your gracious, godly mode;
how fortunate the man who ever
knew your heavenly abode,

your sublime imagery
in a transcendental key.
Blossom in my hymns again,

grace my odes with floral flair,
do not let your glitter wane,
infuse my songs with new-found glare!

CCXII

The song of the sirens is about love and pain,
about a world of dust and roses,
the spider webs of a dubious age,
or the whiteness of spectral marble.

It is his fate to sing the memory of Achaea,
a breath that stirs the gods' holy groves,
a free vent of his boldness innate,
like a race of gleaming chariots.

His audacious and poetic spirit
plunges into a motioning death
and re-emerges in songless times,

conveys his conception of musical flair
as the reverberation of Aegean lore –
his dream in the arms of the Earth!

CCXIII

… and an everlasting fascination
searching for auguries in glistening stars
or in the birds' migrating formation,
an array of flight that attenuates scars.

Belief in primordial arrangements,
in a cryptic melodic design
of the heaven's spherical movements
with which mythical verses align!

But dimensions of life in poleis,
laid out in legend and lore,
at the time of a summer solstice

imparted by spellbound poets in awe,
Achaeans, in the grip of a lunar trance,
flung into a wild Dionysian dance!

CCXIV Flourishing Melos

The response was exhilarating
after such eruption of artistic strength,
the ultimate display of a truly
unfathomable flourish of μέλος,

his intoxication with sea and sun,
with flowering trees and timeless stone,
let his fervour, with glittering flair,
spread a bright reflection of light,

under whose dazzling panorama
earth blossoms swept their scent,
with the intensity of musical rapture,

over Boeotia's Thebes and Eleusis,
over the storied hills of Argolis,
and beyond the Acropolis of Mycenae…

CCXV

The moon, a traveller's companion,
with the gleeful beauty of its light,
spreading joy into the summer night,
keeps me filled with lunar passion.

The morning flowers into life,
a lark sings soaring to the sky;
dimming notions of war and strife,
rouse me again to versify.

But a stranger in a distant land
hear ghostly voices strong and clear
along the spectral alien shore,

where once my Eurydice went,
who takes away infernal fear
of the river Styx and Charon's lore.

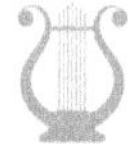

CCXVI

I finally believe I'm sane again,
now that my Elysian dream
has plunged into Scythian gloom,
into the shadow of a starlit night

which I wished went up in flames,
with blinding glare would rustle
the oak tree sacred to Father Zeus
and illumine the *klepsydra,*

the hallowed waters of the Aegean Sea,
imbued with Athena's magical gift
of music in Parnassian metres

gleaming like roses in the rays of the sun,
sing the songs of my juvenescence,
that clung to the strings of my harp,

which once I shared with a godlike throng
on our triumphant return from Troy.

CCXVII

Ideas dispersed by winds of fate
revealing strains of inspiration,
expose contours of dreamlike thought,
the archetypical illumination.

Shades of melancholic Orphean stirs
seep into rapt Eleusinian nights,
seek the portrayal of solemn hymns
and dithyrambic choric chants.

The epic wanderer tracks along
the circuitous paths of destiny
in quest of enigmatic feats;

he who seeks with joy and tears,
soars with ethereal wings
to attain the highest spheres.

CCXVIII

Where are you, divine messenger,
harbinger of bliss, oh, where?
I miss your radiant allure
that the plutonian nights obscure.

With the buoyant sun that rises
beyond the flowering hills of Locris,
almost morning, you come along
the lustrous path of blissful song.

Linger on, O joyous dawn!
One more time let me embrace
your glowing heart, this pristine morn.

Extract love's pain from distant Thrace,
my destiny's most cruel thorn –
I spread out my arms to you, O Eos!

CCXIX

In the deep shade of a cypress grove,
a triumph of word and *melos*
as his lyric imagination flared,
his lyre sang with true abandon.

As if echoing from the Ionian Sea,
the alluring nymph intoned again
a lofty air lauding the waves
like Calypso in Ogygia once.

The treetops stirred in the radiant sunset,
the warbles, chirps, and vernal thrills
of their Orphean language synchronized

with Calliope's panegyric of αγαπη,
of love, that inflamed his poetic fervour,
resonated in his chimeric dreams.

CCXX

A diary of thoughts and dreams
scattered by a mythic wind;
a phase of musings predestined
sounding haunting, tuneful themes.

Sparks of deep-red inspiration,
long-breathed magical elation;
the chords of bygone Orphean harps
reflect the songs of forest larks.

From a Thracian mountain rings,
along the Hebrus' bending shore,
a moving arcane melody

echoing from nature's strings,
sounds the ravine's deepest lore,
the god's primeval memory.

Shall we ban our primordial friendships, the grand
never wooing gods, because the hard steel
that we brought up harshly, has never known their land,
or will a map their whereabouts reveal?

These mighty friends that take away our dead
will nowhere try to restrain our wheels.
Far away we have moved our baths and festive meals;
their slow-moving messengers we had

long overtaken. Lonelier now, we clamber
on one another, without knowing the other's turn,
we no longer arrange a path as a pretty meander

but as clear-cut. Only in boilers still burn
the firers of old and lift ever-heavier hammers.
We, though, keep losing strength like swimmers.

by Rainer Maria Rilke
Sonett an Orpheus XXIV
translated by the author

www.ingramcontent.com/pod-product-compliance
Lightning Source LLC
Chambersburg PA
CBHW032009050726
47590CB00006B/2100